"Her feats are marked with colorful insults, bruising fights, crashing swords, and **daring escapes**. Throughout, Drest is heartened by the imaginary presence of her brothers, whose voices she hears in her head, offering battle tips and a code of conduct. . . . Action-packed at every turn, the story leaves . . . readers hungry for the continuation of the epic adventure."
—*KIRKUS REVIEWS*

"The final **thrilling** scenes rival any video game for action. Drest is a wee lass creating her own legend, and hints at a sequel are welcome."
—*THE PLAIN DEALER*

"Drest is a **likable and headstrong character,** and the composite of various regions in Scotland will appeal to tweens who appreciate atmospheric woodsy settings. Readers will learn, along with Drest, about feudal village life, contemporaneous attitudes toward gender, and the relationship between truth and legend."
—*SCHOOL LIBRARY JOURNAL*

"If you're looking for **action, adventure, and lots of heart** in a story helmed by a strong young warrior, this is an absolute must-read!!! THIS is the book I longed for when I was younger . . . an unforgettable story of family, friendship, and bravery. I loved every page!"
—SARAH GLENN MARSH,
AUTHOR OF *REIGN OF THE FALLEN*

"Drest's story is filled with rich historical detail while allowing Drest and the other characters to stand out in sharply rendered images. **This is a superb children's novel**, perfect for fans of medieval settings."
—GWENDOLYN BALTERA,
BUTTONWOOD BOOKS AND TOYS (COHASSET, MA)

"Medieval Scotland, a quest, **a strong, clever girl**, an injured knight and a magical crow—what's not to like?"
—TRISH BROWN,
ONE MORE PAGE BOOKS (ARLINGTON, VA)

"From the first few pages, I felt like I was curled up in my childhood bedroom, just discovering the magic of stories. **I couldn't tear myself away** from this world until I finished the final page, and long to walk along these paths and through these villages again." —STEPHANIE HEINZ, PRINT: A BOOKSTORE (PORTLAND, ME)

"*The Mad Wolf's Daughter* is a middle grade adventure that we will be recommending to the nines both as a read-aloud and a **great gift** for readers of many ages and dispositions." —KENNY BRECHNER, DEVANEY DOAK & GARRETT BOOKSELLERS (FARMINGTON, ME)

"Drest is the kind of chivalrous, clever, sword-wielding hero that **will have readers singing** Drest's praises and helping her legend to grow. Armed with her wit, a sword much too big for a twelve-year-old-girl, and her stalwart determination, Drest sets forth on a wild and dangerous rescue attempt to save her family before it's too late." —RACHAEL CONRAD, WELLESLEY BOOKS (WELLESLEY, MA)

"Action adventure set in medieval Scotland is rare, especially with such a **fantastic protagonist** as Drest. This story should easily appeal to any reader . . . who enjoys a good quest and some excellent sword fights."
—REBECCA WAESCH, JOSEPH-BETH BOOKSELLERS (CINCINNATI, OH)

"This book is **an exciting and compelling read**, and its stubborn, honorable heroine is set to join the likes of Alanna of Trebond and Aerin of Damar."
—LILLIAN TSCHUDI-CAMPBELL, RED BALLOON BOOKSHOP (ST. PAUL, MN)

AN ENEMY KNIGHT

"Are you alive?" Drest gently lowered the young knight's arm to his side. The chain mail clinked beneath the surcoat. "Can you open your eyes?"

Except for the rising and falling of his chest, the knight didn't move.

That shows he's alive, murmured Nutkin's voice. *Nudge him, lass.*

"I've an idea." Carefully, Drest touched the knight's shoulder. "You wake up, I'll help you get out of this ghost-ridden pit, and then you'll help me find my family. How does that sound?"

The young knight moaned. His eyes flicked open.

Drest shrank. He was defenseless, a wounded man, and needed her help just as much as she needed his. But she had never been so close to someone who wasn't her father or one of her brothers. And he was the enemy.

‹‹-·-››

OTHER BOOKS YOU MAY ENJOY

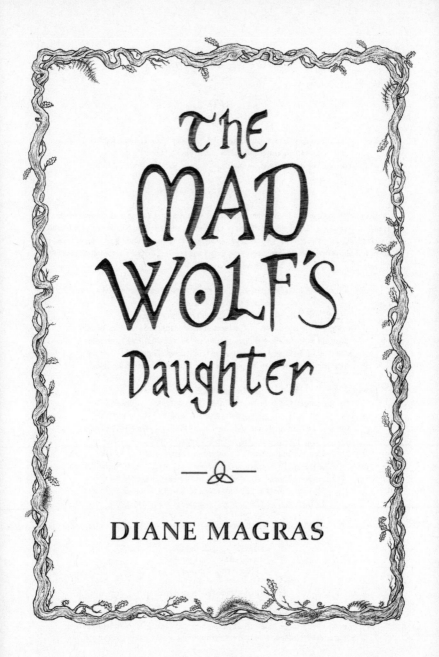

THE MAD WOLF'S Daughter

DIANE MAGRAS

PUFFIN BOOKS

PUFFIN BOOKS
An imprint of Penguin Random House LLC
New York

First published in the United States of America by Kathy Dawson Books,
an imprint of Penguin Random House LLC, 2018
Published by Puffin Books, an imprint of Penguin Random House LLC, 2019

Copyright © 2018 by Diane Magras

THE LIBRARY OF CONGRESS HAS CATALOGED THE KATHY DAWSON BOOKS EDITION AS FOLLOWS:
Names: Magras, Diane, author.
Title: The Mad Wolf's daughter / Diane Magras.
Description: New York, NY : Kathy Dawson Books, [2018] | Summary: "In 1210
Scotland, when invading knights capture twelve-year-old Drest's father, the
Mad Wolf of the North, and her beloved brothers who make up his fearsome
war-band, she sets off to rescue them from the castle prison, taking along
a wounded knight as her captive to trade for her family's freedom"
—Provided by publisher.
Identifiers: LCCN 2017040115 | ISBN 9780735229266 (hardback) |
ISBN 9780735229273 (ebook)
Subjects: | CYAC: Adventure and adventures—Fiction. | Heroes—Fiction. |
War—Fiction. | Knights and knighthood—Fiction. | Middle Ages—Fiction. |
Family life—Scotland—Fiction. | Scotland—History—1057-1603—Fiction. |
BISAC: JUVENILE FICTION / Action & Adventure / General. | JUVENILE FICTION
/ Family / Siblings. | JUVENILE FICTION / Historical / Medieval.
Classification: LCC PZ7.1.M34 Mad 2018 | DDC [Fic]—dc23
LC record available at https://lccn.loc.gov/2017040115

Puffin Books 9780735229280

Map art by Sophie E. Tallis
Designed by Mina Chung
Text set in Dante MT

Printed in the United States of America

1 3 5 7 9 10 8 6 4 2

To Benjamin and Michael

and

in memory of Patricia Harrison

⊶ CONTENTS ⊷

Headland

The Ravine

The Camp

The Main Road

path from the woods

Drest's fire

• Drest's boat

Ridge/chasm

Phearsham Ridge

boggy path

Soggyweald

N

W   E

S

Ancient Scots Pine

Birrensgate

Launceford

crossroads with milestone

Faintree Castle

THE
LOWLANDS

▲ = Dragons' Teeth
-- = Drest's Path
— = Main Road

To the Mad Wolf's lair the brave knights crept,
their hearts in their throats, their swords in their hands;
with a smile on his lips, the Mad Wolf slept,
the Wolf and his sons, the whole band,
aye, the Wolf and his sons, the whole band.

'Twas a battle at which no flags would flap,
though swords would flash and men would fall,
the Wolf would roar and his sons would snap.
Be wary as the beasts-in-the-flesh loom tall,
but be wary of the youngest most of all.

—*Anonymous*, AD *1210, Faintree Castle*

⊷ 1 ⊶

THE SHAPE IN THE WATER

The fog drew back upon the dark sea and revealed a gleaming point like a ship's bow, which seemed to nod at the girl brooding by the glowing bonfire.

"What's that?" Drest leaned forward, her hand on her dagger.

Her elbow dug into the shoulder of her brother Gobin, who lay with his arm slung over the fringe of his coal-black hair.

"Gobin?" She poked him. "Are you awake?"

"Nay."

"There's something in the sea."

"I'm not awake, lass."

"It's something wooden on the waves just past the dragons' teeth."

His eyes flicked open, then closed. "Drest, dear, it's a dream. Lie back. If you want to stay out here with us, you need to sleep."

Drest crept around the fire to Nutkin, Gobin's twin, who lay in almost the same position, except it was his hand, not arm, that held back his black hair.

"I'm not awake, either," Nutkin said, a smile tweaking his lips.

"We come home from war and you're jumping at every sound," muttered Uwen, her youngest brother. "Go to sleep, you crab-headed squid gut, or I'll make you sleep in the cave with the snails."

Drest crawled back to the water's edge. The sea was quiet. The night mist had swept in again. She listened, unmoving, the wind's fingers riffling her short and uneven brown hair.

Grimbol, her father, had always said that no boat or ship could reach their tight, protected cove, that the dragons' teeth—the stones scattered over the harbor—were hungry for wood and men. And no man or devil would dare draw near the headland while her brothers and father were home.

Yet something was there.

Drest left the circle by the fire where her family slept and scrambled up the boulders behind the camp. She climbed over the crumbling stones, dead tree roots, and clumps of gorse, past the crag that looked over the spot of rocky beach where her brothers kept their boats, then higher, until she came to a point where the sea opened up before the headland. Above her rose the path to the cliffs. Behind her lay the caves where her family kept their supplies and slept when it rained. Over the water, the ash-gray fog stretched like smoke. Drest closed her eyes and listened.

Waves, sloshing.

The wind, gently breathing.

Her father and brothers, snoring from below.

A creak.

Not just a creak, but a scrape as well, the rasp of wood on stone in the cove just past the dragons' teeth. She knew that sound: a boat. And it was landing.

Drest flew down the uneven cliff side, blind in the darkness but knowing her way. She pounded back into the camp toward the glow of the bonfire, and dropped to her knees beside her eldest brother.

"Wulfric, there's a boat in the water!"

Wulfric opened his eyes a crack. "What are you saying, lass?"

"A boat. Like one of yours! Lads, get up!"

Heads rose around her. Her father turned over with a growl.

"Our poor wee Drest's had a nightmare," murmured Thorkill, fingering the stone pendant he wore below his curly ginger beard. "Was it Gobin's battle story that kept you awake, lass?"

"Nay, it's not that! I heard a boat." Drest stood, wincing at her brothers' shaking heads. "Lads, I *saw* it!"

"Keep your grub-spotted nightmares to yourself," Uwen mumbled from beside the fire.

Her brothers settled down again, grunting and grumbling, until she was standing alone.

"Why won't you listen? Do I ever tell stories? Lads, there's a *boat* out there."

No one spoke.

Drest opened her mouth, but before she could say anything more, the camp was bright with flames.

⊷ 2 ⊶

INVADERS

They rushed from the shadows, men with massive swords and gleaming shields, their bucket-shaped helms hiding their faces.

Drest's brothers always slept beside their weapons, and were up and armed in seconds, but the invaders had gained an advantage. Nutkin ducked behind the fire and slid to avoid a blade. Wulfric fought from his knees and battered away the enemy who had fallen upon him. Shields crashed together. Swords shrieked against chain mail.

In the middle of it stood Drest, far from her practice sword on the other side of the fire.

A knight dropped his sword and slumped against her. Drest scrambled out from under him, and slammed into another knight's shield, emblazoned with a tree, just like Wulfric's battered one. Drest ducked, twisted, and crawled away. On the loose rocks by the path, she panted. She had never seen a battle, and the sight of it squeezed like an iron band around her chest.

An unfamiliar grasp clamped onto her shoulder.

Drest gave a cry and tried to plunge back into the fight, but an arm gleaming with chain mail grabbed her around the waist and dragged her away, up the path. She lashed out, kicking nothing but rocks and air.

Her captor stumbled. Drest clawed at the stones, then at the hilt of a sword someone had dropped. Her fingers closed on the grip and she swung the blade back. A heavy note rang low and muted against the mail on the man's legs.

"So even a wee wolf like you has teeth." The knight swung down his shield, knocking Drest's sword from her hand.

She kicked, a hopeless gesture. Yet not futile: Her long legs tangled with the invader's, tripping him—and then she was rolling on the ground.

A different arm—just flesh this time—hooked around her ribs and hoisted her up. Drest struggled, but her new captor held her tightly and sprang over the stones, higher and higher, on a path that only her family would have known.

"Get out of here, Drest." Her father's grizzled face looked down into hers. "Make yourself scarce. Don't come out unless I call or until the headland's deserted. Understand? No fighting."

"But Da, what about Uwen?" Her voice came out cowering. Drest cleared her throat. "I'm his battle-mate, am I not? How will he fight without me at his back?"

"I don't want you down there." Grimbol's powerful hand cradled his daughter's chin. "In a fight like this, your battle-mate is the man next to you. And I must be the man next to any of my lads who needs my help. Hide yourself, Drest. Do as I say. You're part of the war-band now and that's my order."

An enemy's sword rose behind him. Grimbol ducked and kicked, sending the knight crashing down the path, then plunged after him, back to the fight.

Holding in a sob, Drest scurried up the uneven cliff side, her father's frantic order forcing her on.

She reached a spot where the sea opened up beyond the cliffs, and stopped. Terror spread over her shoulders like a new skin.

She belonged with Uwen. They weren't ready to fight together, had not perfected Gobin and Nutkin's speed and precision or Wulfric and Thorkill's brute force, but they had achieved a point of trust where they could shuttle courage back and forth. That was the first and most important part of being a true battle-mate, her father always said. It was also the first rule of her father's code of life and war.

Yet Drest could not move, not for the world.

She bowed her head. Uwen had to be safe. Their brothers were with him. The war-band had always returned after battles, sometimes wounded but never gravely so. They would win this attack. They always won.

They had to.

Drest climbed higher, wind gusts whipping at her tunic, until she reached the path to the sea cliffs, the highest point of the headland. On one side, the ravine and its forest loomed, a wall of darkness; on the other crashed the sea. Drest walked along the sea edge, careful to keep far from the ravine. Four years ago, Uwen had fallen there, and crashed to the bottom. It had been a game of chase and they'd been alone, with the war-band away at battle. It had taken a wee Drest hours to drag her brother up through the spindly trees and loose soil.

At the cluster of rocks that looked like a crouching knight when the sun was low, she curled up, as if she were small again and playing a hiding game with Uwen.

As still as stone, Drest listened for the sound of her father's voice. All she could hear from that height was the slosh of the sea.

A whole night seemed to pass as Drest waited, and still her father did not call. She was shifting her position, wondering what she would do if he never called, when another sound came: footsteps against the loose rocks close by.

She almost stood, but stopped herself in time.

A tongue of torchlight had appeared on the path.

Drest ducked. None of her family would carry a torch. She slid down until she found a crack in the stones, and set her eye to it.

Like phantoms from a nightmare, two men in chain mail and white surcoats with a blue tree in the center stepped out of the night fog, their swords glittering in their hands. One was thinner, smaller, and clearly younger, but both reeked of power.

They advanced toward the clump of rocks as if they knew where she was hiding. At the dip in the path where Uwen had tripped, the smaller knight walked on, but the larger one, who carried the torch, stepped in it and stopped.

"This is where you must stay." The larger knight pivoted his back to the cavernous ravine and held his torch to illuminate the cliff before the sea. His face seemed flushed within his chain mail hood. "The ship will wait there."

"I was so close to their camp," the younger knight insisted. He was slender, as wiry as Gobin, with a piece of fair hair sticking out from his chain mail hood. "Why did you keep me from it? Why bring me up here?"

"Because you are young and untested. Sir Oswyn said—"

"But I wish to see the battle!"

"And have the Wolf come down on you with all his might?"

"Do you think I can't defend myself?" The young knight raised his sword and shield. "Will it make you feel better if I brandish these?"

"You'll trip over the rocks more likely," muttered the red-faced knight. "Let me scout. I'll be back faster than you'll know."

Grumbling, the young knight set the tip of his long shield against the stone and leaned upon it. Soon the torchlight disappeared as the red-faced knight strode down the path.

The young man sighed and shrugged. All at once, his shield slipped. With a clatter and scrape, he caught his balance.

"God's bones," he swore softly.

He could have been Gobin playing a joke, pretending to be clumsy. Or maybe he *was* clumsy, as Uwen could be in their practice battles.

Or he was frightened, just as Drest was as she crouched behind the stones.

She knew what would happen next. The red-faced knight would return and tell the young knight that the path was safe. They would approach the camp. They would step into someone's sword—Wulfric's or Thorkill's, or even her father's. The red-faced knight might run, but this one, this clumsy, frightened knight, would join the other knights who lay upon the ground.

And because he made her think of Gobin, Drest sighed.

The young knight flinched. "Who's there?"

Drest froze. He had heard her.

"Who's there, I said."

But he wasn't speaking to Drest.

In a blur, a dark figure sprang toward him from the path, sword aloft in his hand. The young knight raised his shield. But the dark figure's shield struck it hard, and then his sword swung around and landed a solid blow upon the smaller man's chest.

It was as if Uwen were battling Wulfric. And there was no room behind the smaller man to retreat, not on the edge of the ravine.

The dark figure's sword struck again. The young knight escaped the full force of the blow to his shoulder, ducking and pivoting, but his heel landed in the dip in the path.

His attacker seemed to know that. He threw his shield against his opponent's. The young knight dropped his sword. His hand flew to his belt, as if for a dagger.

But he had lost his balance and his attacker had already pulled back.

The young knight disappeared into the ravine in a sliding, scraping, crumbling rush of stone. Tree branches snapped, and leaves rattled. Then all was silent.

The attacker rocked back on his heels and waited. He cleared his throat.

"Are you there?" he called.

The voice stopped Drest cold.

It was the red-faced knight.

⊰ 3 ⊱

GRIMBOL'S ORDER

The red-faced knight picked up the young knight's sword and, with a grunt, threw it toward the sea. There was a clatter, then a muted splash. The knight nodded and descended the path toward the camp.

Trembling, Drest rose. The fight she had witnessed made no sense. In her father's stories about the knights he had known, they had never battled among themselves.

Drest slipped out from her hiding place and crouched on her hands and knees, leaning into the ravine to listen.

Nothing.

He was just a lad. He'd been scared in the dark, then attacked by one of his war-band. Now he lay dead at the bottom of the ravine.

She heard the red-faced knight stumble and swear.

A thin curl of hate rose in Drest. Silent as a ghost, she hastened after him.

Just below the cliff, he stopped to don his white surcoat, then strode on.

The sky had lightened, though the path was still shadowed. Drest hoped the red-faced knight would trip.

But the red-faced knight didn't trip. He veered off to the side, shoving his way through scrub and over stones until he was far from the camp and close to a drop at the sea. Drest followed him on this new, narrow trail.

All at once, the red-faced knight disappeared ahead of her.

Metal rasped against stone. Boots scraped. Paddles splashed in the sea.

A small boat rowed away from the shore toward a huge boat emerging from the darkness.

Drest stared. She had never seen a full ship, only the small war-boats her father and brothers sailed when they went to battle.

Waves slapped against its huge wooden hull. A massive white sail hung limp in the breeze. A series of posts stood on its deck.

Not posts, Drest realized, but knights: a dozen knights with swords and shields, chain mail covering their arms and heads. One knight stood beside a coil of rope.

Yet it wasn't just rope.

Drest froze.

In that coil, her father and brothers were bound: Grimbol lashed to Wulfric, their backs aligned; Gobin and Nut-

14

kin with their heads touching; Thorkill bound to Uwen, his broad shoulders towering over his younger brother's. Grimbol's mouth was moving.

The small boat drew near the ship and the red-faced knight climbed aboard. He spoke to another knight and looked around as if counting. The others were looking too. Drest was so intent on watching that she failed to notice where she stood. Only when the red-faced knight pointed at her did she realize that she was out in the open.

Drest scrambled back over the crumbling stone, then behind a boulder that was just large enough to hide her.

"You missed one!" shouted the red-faced knight in a brutal voice very different from the soft voice he had used with the young knight. "How did you miss one?"

A murmur rose from the bound men. Drest looked out. Her brothers twisted around to see her, their faces tight with concern.

Grimbol raised his chin. "Be like the barnacle and hie thee to the eagle's roost!" His voice echoed down the water and carried over the cove. "The barnacle and the eagle's roost! That's your order now!"

A knight stepped over and gave Grimbol a blow that her father took as if it were a breeze.

Numb, Drest nodded. Be like the barnacle meant to hide,

and the eagle's roost was the highest place she could find. But Drest couldn't flee. She looked out as the red-faced knight marched to the edge of the deck.

His eyes met hers. He seemed to be thinking.

"Shall we set off a boat, sir?" said a knight who had rushed to his side.

"And stumble over these cliffs after him? No, you won't easily catch a cub like that; the men are tired. Sir Oswyn will be anxious to have the rest in prison, where they can't escape. This last one won't go anywhere. We can return and catch him later, and look for what's left of our boy then too."

The red-faced knight stared at Drest as if he knew that she had witnessed his attack upon the young knight. Then he turned away.

"Set sail."

A man in a brown tunic drew up the ship's sail and the enormous vessel began to glide out.

"Nay," the girl whispered.

Her family's faces grew smaller, and smaller. Before long, she could no longer distinguish them from the deck.

In moments, the ship was but a stark shape against the wide, open sea.

Drest sank to her knees and leaned down until her

forehead pressed against the rough, cold stone. Sea wind wrapped over her, chilling her to her core.

They were gone.

She shouldn't have wasted her father's time by the camp. Her brothers had needed him, and she should have escaped that knight on her own. What had all her training been for? To falter in a time of need?

Drest swallowed. Her father had given her an order. She rocked back and wiped her face.

But she didn't run off to hide.

A month ago when the war-band had taken Uwen for his first battle and left her alone, Grimbol had told her to be strong, for she was not like the frail women and girls that his code had sworn them to protect. She was as tough as any of her brothers and didn't need the war-band, he'd said. Yet every night during that month, she had slept not by the water but deep in a cave.

On that first night alone, she'd imagined Uwen's voice, and she'd told him about her sword practice. And the next day and the days after, as she had scampered over the stones and swung her sword and climbed, she'd imagined all her brothers' voices.

Drest closed her eyes.

Are you there, Gobin?

Nothing.

I'm all alone, Gobin. I'm scared. Are you there?

And then, as if her favorite brother were kneeling on the stones beside her: *Of course I'm here, lass.*

Drest slowly inhaled.

Da's order was for you to hide, her brother's voice murmured. *What are you doing here? Get up. You're not a wee helpless maiden, are you?*

Nay, but I don't want to hide. They're not coming back, are they? And what about you?

The wind snapped against her, breaking her concentration.

Drest's eyes flew open and she stared out over the sea.

The ship was gone.

Of course we're gone, you toad-headed minnow, Uwen's voice broke out. *It's a ship. It sails.*

Drest bit her lip, fighting her tears.

Did they hurt you, Uwen?

Nay, not me. But they'll hurt you if you don't hide.

Drest shook her head. That wasn't what Uwen would say.

I was just testing you. It's Da's order, but you've never been in the war-band, so you don't know how to follow it. Aye, why should you follow it? Why don't you follow us instead? If it were me where you're standing, that would have been Da's order: to rescue us.

18

Nay, but it's too far, Uwen.

Would that stop you if we were racing? Come on, Drest. You swim like a seal.

Nay, lad, I can't.

Uwen's voice in her mind let out a snort of disgust. *Go along and hide, then. Be the sniveling, grub-spotted barnacle you are.*

But when Drest rose, she didn't go to hide; she began to run.

She sprinted up to the path, then down, flying, toward the camp. At the last minute, she swerved, dashing over the wide, flat stones to the caves. Her footsteps pounded: past the cave where her family stored their barrels of ale and smoked fish, past the one in which they slept when it rained, then the one that held their silver coins and other stolen goods.

Back up to the cliffs, then down the path that led to the sea caves on the shore. Drest scrambled over the wet stones, splashing in the waves, and climbed up a short cliff. She crawled to the path, and started to run again.

Running always helped calm her. It helped her think. She always ran after she argued with Uwen, sometimes in a race, sometimes alone. She ran when she failed in training battles with Gobin or throwing games with Thorkill. She had run to keep away loneliness during that awful month when Uwen had gone with the war-band. And so Drest ran until she could no longer run. She collapsed panting on the lookout point.

Do you feel better now? It was Thorkill's voice. *Look at how the sun sparkles on the waves. Do you hear the gulls crying? It's peaceful.*

Tears stung Drest's eyes. *Nay, it's not peaceful, not with you roped up.*

Don't weep, lass. Thorkill's voice was tender. *Go down to our camp and see what you can find. It may give you an idea of what to do.*

Drest stared at the path, and shuddered. But soon she was on her feet and walking down.

The ground was full of broken swords: on their sides, on the rocks, or driven into the pebbles. Scraped-up stones showed where the battle had been fiercest. Drest could not take her eyes from the paths on which the knights had dragged her brothers to the sea.

The crackling bonfire that Grimbol had told them never to let burn out was only embers now.

Drest knelt by the blackened wood. When her brothers were home, this was where they had gathered every night to feast and tell stories. Here she had sat rapt as her brothers had spoken of blows and broken shields in battle, of the swiftness that had saved their lives. She'd grabbed her own share of ale and meat and gone to sit with her father, who'd tuck her under his rough, warm arm as he told his tales of castle sieges in the days when he'd fought among knights of another war-band.

She had only felt alone once before in her life, when Uwen had gone, but this time, she truly was.

You're never alone with your sword by your side, said Gobin's voice. *Remember Da's code: Always carry a weapon. So where's your weapon, Drest?*

Drest looked around. Hers was only a practice sword, a worthless piece of scrap, but what Gobin said was true.

She found it soon enough, but only its hilt with a sliver of the broken blade remaining.

Now it's truly a piece of scrap, came Uwen's voice. *See if you can find mine. I'll let you borrow it just this once.*

Drest searched, but every sword she found was broken.

As she kicked at a shattered weapon that had been thrown into the sea's foam, something glittered deep, among the dragons' teeth.

Go look at that sword, murmured Wulfric's voice.

Drest slipped off her boots and hose and waded into the sea. The water slithered like a frozen breath up her ankles,

21

then up to her knees, and higher. Finally, she reached the sword. It was unbroken, undamaged, its pommel thick with ridges like the headland's cliffs.

It was Borawyn, Wulfric's sword, the only named sword among the war-band's weapons. A sword that had never lost a battle—until now.

Drest drew the blade from the water and held it high, her arm shaking beneath its weight. The sword sparkled in the early sun.

It was waiting for you, said Wulfric's deep voice.

Did you throw it in the waves for me?

I threw it in so our enemies wouldn't steal it. It will bring you luck, lass. Use it well.

Aye, use it well, chimed in Uwen, *and use it soon; this rope is digging into me.*

Drest squinted at the sea. *How do you expect me to use it for that, you snail-brained cabbage? I can't cut your rope from here.*

Use it as you come after us, you onion-eyed pig's bladder.

Drest stared at the water. *Could* she go after them?

Of course you can, scoffed Uwen. *You have a sword, don't you?*

Drest sloshed back to the desolate camp and put on her hose and boots. In one direction, the sea stretched far and empty; in the other, beyond the caves and the paths, lay the ravine, marked by the sea cliffs on one end and a cliff no one could climb on the other.

Drest hesitated. She had never been off the headland. Even if she could scale the ravine's slick cliff, she didn't know where the woods at its top went or what path she should take through them. There had to be a way, but she didn't know what she was looking for.

Drest found an abandoned scabbard and a sword-belt on the ground. She buckled the belt over her hips as tight as she could, fitted the scabbard in its loops, and slipped Borawyn in. A year ago, she would have been too small to carry that sword, but her legs had grown and she could stand easily against its weight upon her hip.

All right, lads, Drest thought. She took a deep breath. *One of you needs to tell me the path. How do I get off the headland?*

You could go through the waves, said Nutkin's voice, *but the boats are smashed; you know they are because that's where the knights landed.*

You could go through the woods, said Gobin's voice, *except the ravine will be in your way. And I don't think even you can climb that cliff.*

She might; she's like a spider.

Aye, I know, Nutkin, but even a spider can't climb sheer rock.

I'll go by the sea, Drest thought. *I'll find a way. How about your fishing boat, Nutkin? Did they find that?*

Nay, I wouldn't think so. That's a fine idea, lass. Aye, go by the fishing boat. Only, you'll need to find out where we've been taken.

Can you not tell me?

Nay, lass, being only part of your imagination as I am. Nutkin's voice laughed. *But that's all right; you've another man you can ask for the way. He might not be dead.*

And then, all at once, Drest remembered the young knight.

⤙ 4 ⤚

EMERICK

The young knight's shield had caught on a branch where it hung like a flag. Drest clambered past it on the trail of raked soil and fallen stones, Wulfric's sword thumping against her hip. She found the knight at the bottom of the ravine, sprawled on his back, his right arm twisted at an unnatural angle.

He was smaller than she had remembered. Fair-haired, fine-boned, unlike any of her brothers, though he still seemed to be close to Gobin's height. His eyes were closed.

Panting from her unsteady descent, Drest bent over him. There was no blood on his mouth or nose—a good sign.

"Are you alive?" Drest gently lowered the young knight's arm to his side. The chain mail clinked beneath the surcoat. "Can you open your eyes?"

Except for the rising and falling of his chest, the knight didn't move.

That shows he's alive, murmured Nutkin's voice. *Nudge him, lass.*

"I've an idea." Carefully, Drest touched the knight's shoulder. "You wake up, I'll help you get out of this ghost-ridden pit, and then you'll help me find my family. How does that sound?"

The young knight moaned. His eyes flicked open.

Drest shrank. He was defenseless, a wounded man, and needed her help just as much as she needed his. But she had never been so close to someone who wasn't her father or one of her brothers. And he was the enemy.

He tried to prop himself up. His hand slipped. He tried again, but he fell back just as quickly, the weight of his chain mail dragging him down.

Drest mustered her courage. "You need to take off that metal tunic."

The young knight leaned on his side. With some effort, he raised himself on his elbow and faced Drest. "Who in God's name are *you*?"

Drest scrambled to her feet.

"Wait," said the young knight. "Don't leave. I'm only asking who you are."

She was far enough away that he couldn't grab her, even if he were to fall forward at his full height. Drest steadied herself on a tree and raised her chin. "I'm part of the war-band."

"Grimbol's war-band?" The young knight sighed. "You've

thrown me down here and now you come to slay me. Before you do, tell your father that I have something to say to him."

Tears sprang to Drest's eyes. "Your toad-witted people took my da and my brothers. And I didn't throw you down here; one of your own men did."

The young knight's voice quivered. "What a filthy lie. Those are my most faithful men."

His despair gave Drest courage. She crept closer. "Maybe some of them, but not the one who was up on the cliff with you. I watched him fight and push you down here." The mist was thickening around them. Drest looked back to find the trail. "Do you know where they've taken my da?"

The young knight's eyes widened. "To Faintree Castle. Do you even know who we are?"

"Nay," said Drest, "why should I?"

"Everything in this part of the lowlands—including this headland—belongs to Faintree Castle."

"Is that the truth? Strange. I've always known that my da owned this headland and *all* the lowlands."

Drest was about to go on, but stopped at the sound of Nutkin's voice in her head: *Boasting like that isn't going to help you find the castle, lass.*

"I beg your pardon." Drest took another step toward the

knight. "I need to find your castle. Can you show me the way?"

"No, I don't think I can." The young knight used the elbow that supported him to push himself up still farther. But as he tried to rise, his face seized in a spasm of pain, and he collapsed onto his back again.

Drest hadn't seen a man in such pain before. Her brothers had grinned as they tended one another's wounds, making few sounds.

Now's your chance, whispered Nutkin. *Give him a wee bit of help and win him over.*

Drest crawled to the young knight's side. "You've got to take off your metal tunic, like I said." She leaned forward to tap it, but darted back as his hand began to close on her arm.

"I wasn't trying to grab you," the wounded man said weakly. "I can't move."

"I'll help you move if you promise not to grab me."

"How can I move unless I grab you?" Struggling, he propped himself up on his elbow again. "And I can't remove my hauberk; it's all that's holding me together."

The worry in his voice persuaded Drest to crawl close once more.

"Here," the young knight said, and held out his hand. "Take this and pull."

Drest took that hand. His firm grip startled her, but she held on and tugged.

He hissed a sharp gasp. "No, not like that. I'm—there's something ripped near that arm. In my chest."

Drest let him go and stepped back, trembling. The mist was growing thicker. Soon she wouldn't be able to find the trail.

"You're right," he said. "I can't move with my hauberk. Can you help me take it off?"

"I don't know," Drest said. "I've never seen one of those things." Cautiously, she returned to his side.

"It won't take much. Cut off my surcoat first. Then roll up the hauberk from the bottom."

Drest's dagger cut easily through the surcoat, and the cloth fell aside. But the chain mail was hard to roll. It was damp against her fingers from the fog. Soon it became warm, and damp from something else. Drest tried not to look. But it was not difficult to guess at the state of the young knight's injuries by his suppressed gasps.

"Almost finished." Drest rolled the armor all the way up his chest, revealing the spotted tunic underneath. Her stomach pitched.

"Don't pause. Just take it off." The young knight spoke between clenched teeth.

At last, it was off. Drest left the hauberk in a heap behind the wounded man's head. Gently, as she had carried Uwen four years ago, she eased the young knight to his feet and slipped his left arm, his better arm, over her shoulder. He was taller than she, but not by all that much, and less heavy than Uwen had been for her smaller self.

"Thank you," he said. "I would never have expected help from one of Grimbol's beasts. How strange you are. What's your name?"

"Drest. You're stranger than I am, you know. What's yours?"

"Of course he'd name you after a savage Pict. My name is Emerick. You're far kinder than most bloodthirsty villains I've met." He glanced at her face, and started. "God's bones, you're a lass."

"You say that as if I'm a three-headed goose. Have you never seen a lass before?"

"I've seen many, but never one like you. What was your mother? A banshee?"

Drest scowled. "I don't know who my mother was. But if you insult her again, I'll drop you."

"Banshees are much honored at Faintree Castle," the young knight murmured. "So are savage Picts." He shivered. "The fog is growing."

"It's always like that down here." Drest led him toward the trail down the cliff, stepping carefully over the roots and moss, Borawyn thumping on her hip. "Since I just helped you and I don't plan to drop you, will you tell me where the castle is?"

The wounded man clung to her, inhaling sharply at every step. "I'll do better than that: I'll lead you to Faintree Castle, and I won't let them hang you when we arrive."

Together they stumbled over the moss to the cluster of trees that marked the trail. Emerick leaned heavily on her as she struggled up the bank. When they reached the top and stood in the foggy sun, Drest had to catch her breath.

"I wonder where the men have gone." Emerick's voice was faint. "Are you sure they've sailed?"

"Aye, they've taken away my family, just as I said."

"How could they leave without me? That would be strictly against their orders."

He looked toward the sea, frowning.

"*I* disobey orders," Drest said. "See, one of my da's is to slay all intruders. Shall we go down to the camp? I'll get you fixed up and then we can go after my family."

‹‹ 5 ››

THE TALISMAN

Drest eased Emerick down by the bonfire's ashes, the tip of Borawyn's scabbard scraping on the pebbles as she knelt. Everything seemed possible now. She had a guide who could lead her to the place he'd mentioned— Faintree Castle—where she'd find the prison. She knew all about castle prisons from her father's stories. As soon as she freed the war-band, they'd slip down to the sea and swim to freedom. She just had to keep the young knight alive until she reached the castle.

With a small chunk of steel from a broken sword and a stone from her pouch—every one of her brothers carried the same—Drest made a spark and built up the fire with the invaders' burnt-out torches that scattered the ground. As the flames grew, she fetched a bundle of bandage cloths that her father kept dry in a cave, and also a bucket of rain-water.

Drest struggled back to the fire, her sword knocking

against the heavy bucket. The wounded man's eyes were closed when she reached him, his eyelids shining faintly blue against his skin.

"Hold still." Drest had watched how her brothers helped one another when they'd come home after battles. The first task was to examine the wounds.

Two swipes of her dagger, and his padded tunic came off. Beneath it lay another shirt, this one linen and slick. Drest cut carefully, holding her breath, turning away when her nausea grew too great. At last, his chest and shoulders were bare. Drest ladled water over them with her hands and, wincing, looked back.

Bruises had already begun to blossom all over his pale chest, clustered where the stones and trees had struck him. There were only a few bleeding wounds: on his shoulder where the red-faced knight had cast a glancing blow, and on his ribs, a dark and ugly one, where the red-faced knight had struck the hardest. Drest ladled more water on him, then bound his wounds with bandages and covered it all with a rumpled dry tunic she'd found.

The young knight was shivering, and so was Drest, though the sun was well risen and the fire was high. She went in search of blankets and returned with her arms full of them. Soon she had the wounded man fully draped.

"Your brothers have taught you some useful skills, it seems," Emerick murmured. "I never thought I'd find a creature like you here."

"What did you think you'd find?" Drest folded a blanket under his chin.

"Nothing but bloodthirsty villains."

"How do you know I'm not one?"

They ate from Grimbol's store of smoked fish and ale, speaking little, facing the sea where the knights' ship had come and gone.

When they finished, Emerick tore his gaze from the water. "How brave are you? I trust that you hold that quality as strongly as does any lad."

Drest raised her head. She didn't like his tone: bitter and haughty, as if he were about to scold her. "What does *that* mean?"

"It means I am willing to rely on you." Emerick reached between the blankets. Drest flinched, but he didn't draw his dagger; instead he drew out a thick black disk, small enough to fit neatly in the palm of his hand.

"If I die, take this to Faintree Castle and tell the guard what has happened."

It was a black wooden talisman with a tree carved in its center. Drest closed her fingers around it. At once, she saw its use: a means to get inside the castle. She had the start of a plan already.

"I'll use it if I need it," Drest said, slipping the talisman into the pouch at her belt, "but you'll be alive when we reach your castle. Where is it?"

"Down the coast. It's many days by land but by sea it's little more than a night."

Drest froze. "We've but a night, then."

"To catch the ship? You wouldn't be fast enough."

"Nay, to catch my da and my brothers. Before—before anything happens to them."

Emerick was quiet. "You say that as if you love them."

"Of course I love them; they're my family. How much time do I have to rescue them? Is it just a night?"

He shook his head. "It's Lent now, so they won't be hanged until the morning after Easter. That gives you five days."

You can do it, Uwen's voice whispered in her mind. *Five days is forever to a bat-headed weasel like you.*

She found Nutkin's old fishing boat up past the camp on the shore near the cave where her family kept their food. The hull looked sound. The mast was strong. And the sail had been untouched by mice.

Drest loaded the small boat with smoked fish and ale

and dragged it back to the camp and into the water. Steadying the boat, she helped Emerick climb in, then launched the craft.

It had been two years since Nutkin had showed her the watery path between the dragons' teeth and how to slip unscathed between them. But Drest remembered. With her arms in the water, she grabbed each point of stone beneath the waves and used it to pull the boat through. The first two stones scraped the hull and another thumped it hard. But soon the boat was sliding noiselessly between them. Then with a final push, they were in open water.

Drest raised the sail. The cloth snapped, catching a gust of wind. With that, the little boat shot out of the cove. Soon they were far from the dragons' teeth.

She tied down the sail to keep their course, and sat back. She was feeling better. They were on the water and would be at Faintree Castle by night. She would have five whole days to figure out her plan and free her family.

"I did it," Drest said. "I guided the boat out. It's my first time doing it alone."

She looked over to where Nutkin had always sat in the stern. The young knight was in her brother's place, glaring at her.

"We did it," Drest said. "Aren't you glad? We're on our way."

"Good."

"You could find a better word than that."

The small craft sped as if weightless in the pull of the wind.

Drest fidgeted. She had never sailed beyond the cove. She had never sailed as far as they were already. She had never sailed without one of her brothers.

And then she noticed a finger's length of water sloshing around her boots.

"Is there a leak in your craft?" said Emerick.

Before she could answer, a gust of wind shoved the boat hard, plunging one side into the waves.

"Can you straighten this?" cried the young knight. "We're about to sink!"

"Nay, it's just how it leans when the wind's too strong. You've never sailed before, have you?" Drest scrambled up the hull to loosen the sail. She had just untied the knot when the boat gave a shudder.

A thunderous crack shook the water.

Drest's hands were still on the rope as the boat fell into pieces around her.

6

THE WATER RAT

The sea hit Drest like a blow, freezing her mind, her breath, her movement—but only for an instant. In the next, the cold had seeped throughout her body and she felt one with the ocean.

She opened her eyes, ignoring the sting that always came with seawater, and launched toward the surface. She had to swim up and think of nothing but her strokes and kicks.

With a gasp, Drest broke through the waves.

All around, bundles of smoked fish and jugs of ale were floating away. Slabs of the boat followed them. She saw no sign of the young knight.

"Blast," muttered Drest, and gulped down a mouthful of seawater. She spat it out. "Emerick? Where are you?"

She saw him then, clinging helplessly to a loose plank. Pain and terror creased his face.

A wave sloshed against Drest's head. She kicked to rise above it—and caught a glimpse of the shore: not close, but not too far.

It's a good thing you're a rat. It was Uwen's voice. *Because rats can swim.*

"Help me," murmured the wounded man, the sea swallowing his words.

Drest glanced back at him. The young knight was sinking on the plank he'd secured. In seconds, he'd be gone.

He's told you where the castle is, whispered Gobin's voice. *And you have the talisman that will let you in. Wouldn't it be easier to swim for shore now? Don't forget: He's our enemy.*

Aye, that's true, said Nutkin, *but how's she going to find us, lad? She's going to have to take the woods, and she doesn't know the path. Our enemy knows that way, not our wee Drest. I don't think you can leave him yet, lass.*

"Listen, Drest." Emerick tried to pull himself higher on the plank, but it wobbled beneath his weight. He slid back into the water. "If you take me to the castle, you can have one of your brothers for me."

A wave cut off his next words, choking him.

"Do you mean it?" called Drest. "How about two of them? Or all of them?"

The next wave swallowed him entirely.

Two good strokes took Drest to Emerick's side. She grabbed on to the plank and tried to straighten it, but the motion made it tip.

Fetch the ropes and mast, said Nutkin's voice. *You've no choice but to pull him to shore.*

The mast was drifting away on the waves. Drest swam for it, and soon was clutching its smooth, slippery wood. She kicked hard to get back to Emerick, the sail trailing behind her like a single white wing.

The water was up to his chin. Drest grabbed his good arm and slung it over the mast.

"Hold tight."

With the rope looped around her arm and shoulder, giving herself enough slack for a distance between her and the wounded man, Drest began to swim.

Towing a man wasn't easy, but Drest and Uwen had taken turns towing the fishing boat and she knew how to time her strokes with the waves. Borawyn glided alongside her, kept aloft in the water by the current, the sword-belt holding it securely.

Several times Drest glanced back to see Emerick hanging over the mast, his face hidden by the sail.

"Give a call if you're slipping," she shouted, and grimly swam on, the rope straining against her shoulder.

At last, Drest reached the dragons' teeth by the shore and stood. The water was up to her chest. She hauled the mast close until Emerick was within reach, then pried loose his grip.

"We've made it," Drest said. "And you're alive, aren't you?"

The wounded man's eyes opened. "Barely."

Drest slipped under his good arm and hoisted his weight onto her shoulder again. Clinging to his waist to steady him, she staggered through the last of the sea and up the shore.

On the pebbles and scraps of sand, Drest stopped. Her arms and legs were numb from her swim.

"I need to lie down," whispered Emerick.

"We can't rest here."

"I cannot go farther. I need to breathe."

"You're not going to have a chance to breathe if we don't go in. Look—the tide's coming."

Drest tightened her grip around him and together they hobbled up the bank, then over the bone-white roots sticking out of the soil until they were among a thick cluster of pines.

An unfamiliar forest hung before them. Drest remembered her father's stories of what roamed the woods beyond the headland: bandits with brutal ways and no mercy to any man.

But she had no choice. Drest helped Emerick walk deeper among the trees. The damp scent of soil and wood rose around her, mingling with the eerie sense that someone was watching.

⊷ 7 ⊶

WORDS WITH THE ENEMY

"Wait." Drest wiped her face free of the streams of water dripping from her short hair.

Emerick leaned against a scaly trunk. "If we go inland a little more, we'll be out of the wind."

"You said I could trade you. For one of my brothers." Her voice trembled, but Drest stood firm.

"Yes," the wounded man murmured. "Any one you like. Pick your favorite."

"All of them."

The young knight shook his head. "You know I can't do that. But I can promise you one brother. And mercy. For you."

"I don't want mercy; I want all my brothers back."

Emerick's eyes fixed on her with a peculiar intensity. "Mercy is worth more than you realize. I could give you a new life: a home at the castle, proper clothes to wear, a warm bed to sleep on at night. And no rope around your throat."

"I don't need a new life." Though Drest flinched at the thought of the rope. "I've a home at the headland with a bed by the water, and I know how to make my own fire to keep warm. I don't want this mercy and just one of my brothers in a trade. Give me all of them, and I'll make sure you reach the castle alive."

The young knight's eyes hardened. "All of them will die if you don't agree to my terms. One brother and mercy."

That's not fair! snarled Uwen's voice.

A tickle of anger wove through Drest's fatigue, pulling harder and harder—and abruptly snapped. "You'll agree to *my* terms: I'll not let you die, but only if you'll help me trade you for *all* my family."

"Even if I were willing, no one at the castle would accept such a trade!"

Drest wiped her face again. "I hope you can make them accept it. Because I'll leave you in these woods if you can't."

She had spoken the bold words without thinking.

The young knight's face became stiff. "How dare you. For that, I take away my offer. I'll give you nothing, not even one man."

"Then I'll leave you."

"Do," said Emerick. "My men will find me, and when they find *you*, they'll hang you with the rest of your wretched family."

"Your men won't come back. Maybe the knight who tried to slay you, but that won't do you any good."

THE MAD WOLF'S DAUGHTER

Emerick's eyes narrowed. "That's a lie. One of your brothers tried to slay me."

"Is it a lie because I said so? Then am I lying when I tell you they were worried about the orders of some Sir Oswyn when they left?"

The young knight reddened. "Oswyn didn't give the orders for this battle; Lord Faintree did."

"They were talking about some Oswyn and they were more worried about what he would think than whether you were alive or not." Drest pretended to look out at the water. "I don't see anyone. Wait, there's a duck. I think it's coming to save you."

"Why *don't* you leave me? Go, find the castle by yourself. Bide your luck alone, and I shall bide mine."

She almost did. She almost stomped into the woods and left him standing there on the bank by the sea. But the young knight's words—and the word *alone* in particular—made Drest pause.

She went back to the young knight's side and pulled his limp arm over her shoulder. "You for one of my brothers. Let's go back to that."

"Not even one. I warned you."

But he leaned on her as they stumbled together into the woods.

◄◄•►►

It was dark by the time they had gone deep enough to escape the cold sea air. Drest would have plodded farther, but the young knight, despite his bluster, could barely walk. She listened to his ragged breath against her hair and knew that if they kept going, he'd soon collapse.

Though her brothers had always provided for her—bringing ale and smoked meat home from war, cooking hearth bread on the bonfire—Drest had also always known how to find food, heat, and water no matter where she was on the headland. Wulfric had shown her how to rip shreds of bark from living trees as tinder for a fire. Thorkill had helped her sharpen a stick with a dagger and then trained her to throw that stick powerfully and quickly enough to take down a squirrel in mid-jump. Gobin had taught her how to follow animal and bird footprints to catch prey; Nutkin how to find fresh water by signs on bark, grass, or leaves. On days when they had been tired of eating the fish they caught in the shallow water or the grain their father brought home from war, Uwen and Drest had hunted together in the ravine, joined through excitement, need, and fear in equal measures.

Drest set Emerick into a pile of leaves and gathered a handful of bark to make a fire. The stone in her pouch was wet, so she had to scrabble about for a dry one. None she found on the forest floor were all that dry.

A spark rose, then went out. Another blow of steel to stone, another dying spark. It took four tries, but at last, the bark ignited. She fed the flame slowly with slivers of wood and imagined her eldest brother's stern, strong face.

A little higher, Drest, or you'll have it fade before you can grow warm. In her mind, Wulfric stroked his corded brown beard. *And you'll want to be warm. First rule of battle: Prepare yourself with weapons. Second: Control your anger as its own fine blade. Third: Get your rest, and stay warm, for the field will be cold and you will often need to draw on the memory of that warmth.*

From the pile of leaves where she'd left him, Emerick shifted. "I can't move," he said, his voice tight with panic. "Come help me. I'm cold. I can't move to be near the fire."

"Stop complaining, you crab-legged gull's bottom," Drest muttered under her breath. "You can move enough to talk, can you not?" She slid another stick into the fire—too hard, spraying sparks over the dirt circle she had mounded to keep the flames in place—and approached the wounded man.

All her work at the camp had been for naught: His bandages had come undone and were loose wet clumps beneath his tunic. Drest stood helpless.

"The fire," Emerick moaned. "Please. I'm so cold." A series of rapid shudders ran down his body like fever.

Drest closed her eyes. Her father would have told her to

46

trust in the talisman and find the castle on her own. She had wasted enough time.

As if he could hear what she was thinking, the wounded man spoke. "A trade," he whispered. "One man."

"You've said that before and taken it back." But Drest stood uncertain. His breath caught as he inhaled. Her brothers had never been so injured.

She hoisted him up on her shoulder again. Taking on all his weight now, Drest staggered with the young knight toward the fire. The flames were crackling and warm. As she tried to set him down gently, her sleeve caught on his dagger's crossguard and ripped.

Drest freed the cloth, but didn't let the fabric go at once. She didn't want to give up her tunic, but the sleeves might serve as bandages. She pulled at one, and the frayed spots around the elbow tore easily. She tore the other.

The sleeves were still wet with salt water, which made Emerick moan as Drest held them against his wounds. But they staunched the blood when she tied them on with the thin ropes she had used before. Afterward, Emerick lay with his face against the ground, breathing hard.

"Are you hungry?" Drest said. "Give me a moment and I'll fetch us something to eat."

The wounded man didn't answer.

Drest went off to hunt.

She listened for sounds and tried not to think about the bandits of her father's stories. Crouching in the dark, following the quiet shuffle of what she hoped was a hare, Drest imagined Uwen beside her.

Movement flashed near the ground. She crept nearer, then nearer. It *was* a hare, hunched over and still; she could just make out its shape. Drest waited, then pounced, seizing it with her strong fingers.

Emerick was asleep when Drest returned with their meal. She reached for her dagger—then remembered it was gone, forgotten by the fire at the camp.

But Emerick had one.

Drest knelt beside the young knight's sleeping form and lifted the corner of his tunic to reveal his dagger's sheath. Without a sound, she slipped his knife free.

It didn't feel like her dagger; it was heavier. When she had it in the firelight, she saw why: Glittering blue gems were stamped into the pommel, and the blade was thick and strong.

It cut well. Drest skinned and cleaned the hare and soon had it on a spit above the fire. She wiped the dagger against the leaves and began to slip it back into its sheath on Emerick's belt.

Are you as blind as a rotting fish? Uwen's voice seemed to explode in her head. *That's your enemy's dagger! Where's your dagger? Back at the camp. Do you really want to give that one up?*

Emerick was still asleep, his eyelids trembling faintly.

Drest stepped away, taking care to make no sound. She began to slide the dagger into her own empty sheath, but stopped: That would be too obvious. Drest thought, then loosened her belt, slid it up under her tunic, and tightened it by her ribs. The dagger fit neatly in its sheath against her stomach.

He's never going to find it there. Uwen laughed.

Drest settled by the fire while the hare cooked. She was following Wulfric's advice—weapons, a fire, controlling her anger—as if there really were a battle ahead.

Fatigue from her swim rushed over her, and Drest closed her eyes.

Five days.

She saw her family in ropes, her father's fierce stare, the worried gazes of her brothers. Were they off the ship yet? Was Uwen frightened?

The forest sounds seemed loud around her: leaves whispering in the wind, trunks creaking as they swayed; the hare dripping juices that made the fire spit and crackle; and the wounded knight drawing in his breath as if pulling a burden over a dry, rocky beach.

A branch snapped.

Drest's eyes flew open.

A shape was moving at the edge of the forest past the fire, a flicker of darkness, then nothing.

Drest bolted to her feet, fumbling for Borawyn's grip.

Everything was still.

Except for something breathing in the distance.

A very large bandit or a very small sea. Uwen's voice, scoffing.

Drest tried to scoff too, but her throat caught. *I need you, Uwen. I need you here right now.*

Then Nutkin's voice was in her mind: gentle and soothing. *Nay, you don't need him, lass. Not when you have your sword and your courage.*

Not when you have us, Gobin's voice added.

Drest straightened. If she had closed her eyes, she could have sworn that the twins were there, one on either side of her, their swords drawn, their black hair dangling in their faces as they leaned close.

This is what we'll do, lass: I'll go off to the left as if I've something to do in the bushes. Nutkin will tell you that he's going to give me a scare and will get up and leave on the other side. You sit here looking wide-eyed and innocent, and pretend that your sword is too heavy to lift—

Another stick broke. Drest tugged Borawyn out of its scabbard. The massive blade wobbled in the firelight.

There you are, lass. But stand as if you can't hold it. Then when he comes at you, thinking you're helpless, bring it up.

When who comes at me, Gobin? Tension crept into her shoulders.

The bandit, of course.

But—but can't you and Nutkin—can you not circle in on him?

Her brother's laugh was faint. *I wish we could, lass, but we're in ropes, and nearly at the castle. You need to get to the castle too, you know. And soon.*

It was as if a knife had pricked her. Drest almost dropped the sword.

She's struggling. Nutkin's voice. *You've asked too much. Drest, lass, listen to me: Sheathe your sword and run. You're faster than any of us. Take that bandit on a chase he won't forget.*

Aye, said Gobin's voice, *he's right. You'll manage that sword soon enough, but for now, use your natural talent: those swift feet.*

He's just behind the bushes.

Quick, lass.

Drest slipped her brother's sword back into its scabbard.

Emerick stirred.

She looked at him.

He's your enemy, whispered Gobin's voice. *And you haven't time. Go.*

With a final glance at the wounded man, Drest dashed into the woods.

❈ 8 ❈

THE BANDIT

The trees came fast at Drest as she ran. She whipped between them, darkness shrouding everything before her. Twigs scraped her arms and roots tripped her feet, yet she kept her balance with her speed and her fear, which, like a torch, led her on through the endless pattern of branches and trunks.

Then a moss-covered tree on the forest floor seemed to reach up. Drest leaped, but badly. The old wood caught her ankle, pulling her down into an embrace of branches soft with decay.

Drest lay still, her heartbeat thumping in her ears like footsteps, her breath burning in her chest. She closed her eyes and tried to force her body to calm, just as she had when Uwen was chasing her and she needed to hide without making a sound. She thought of the sea and how it breathed: slowly in, slowly out, over and over.

When Drest opened her eyes, she heard real waves slapping against the shore. The sea was nearby.

She rose and started toward that sound. The presence at the edge of the woods had been but a nightmare, a trick of her exhaustion. There was no bandit, only the woods, only the night and the sea.

Fallen branches slippery with moss littered her path. Shells glowed white among them. The scent of the muddy brine was pungent.

As the watery sound became louder, Wulfric's voice flashed through Drest's mind:

Careful.

Drest stopped. She was standing on a grassy bank with the sea just beyond. She was about to turn back, but her eye caught a movement in the trees.

On the bank's other side, in the shadows, stood a man.

The sea sent a rush of waves toward the shore, its sound nearly swallowing a voice: soft and slippery like a fish's belly.

"Are you alone, girl?"

The figure disappeared into the trees.

Drest drew her sword, her heart pounding anew.

Don't try it. Gobin's voice was urgent. *Remember what we said before? What can you do best? Run. So run like a hare!*

Drest sheathed her sword and broke into a sprint.

A crash sounded behind her, followed by cracking twigs. The bandit wasn't as fast as she was, but the noise of his pursuit was coming closer. There was no doubt now that he was real.

Drest ran with new strength. Twice she had to grab trees when she lost her footing, but she kept on her feet.

She wanted to imagine she was running with Uwen. They had often made up stories of being hunted by cruel foes to urge each other to run ever faster.

Drest swallowed a sob. If only Uwen were there! Together, they would have taken but seconds to devise a plan to trap the bandit. Or Gobin and Nutkin, who would have circled him and then gone in. Or Thorkill, who would have stood with her, and let loose an arrow. Or Wulfric, who would have marched into the woods and felled the bandit with one blow.

Or Grimbol, who would have torn that bandit to pieces.

Drest slowed to duck under a low branch, then changed her mind and scrambled over it, Borawyn's scabbard slapping against her leg. The bandit's panting came from behind. He'd had less trouble on Drest's path than she, which could only mean that he knew these woods well.

"Wait, girl," the slippery voice called from behind.

Drest did not stop running.

"Are you alone, I asked. I don't think your brothers are

here. Only you and me. Don't you want to talk to another lonely soul?"

Sticks crashed behind her. The bandit was drawing close again.

Drest veered between trees, launching in a new direction. She flew through branches and over thick moss, ducking and weaving.

And then a different voice called in the distance, not very far away: "Drest? Drest, where are you?"

She broke into the tiny clearing where the fire was almost out. In the dark, she could barely see Emerick, leaning against a tree.

"There's a bandit. He's on my heels. We've got to hide."

Drest put her shoulder under the wounded man's arm and drew him into the woods, away from the sea, on the faint trail she had followed when hunting the hare, then beyond. Behind her, the slippery voice swore, then was quiet.

"Here," Drest whispered, lowering Emerick into a clutch of ferns. She curled up against him. "Don't move."

Emerick stifled a groan as he leaned back. "I wish I had my sword."

"Stop talking. And shut your eyes so the whites don't show."

Drest shut her own eyes, and tensed.

A foot stepped over a branch near her head. Drest, whose games with Uwen had trained her to listen, heard the faint rustle that the bandit made as he drifted into the woods, and heard when he was gone.

But his soft, slippery voice spoke again, even closer. "Where are you, girl? I've seen you grow up, but I don't know your name."

Drest lay as if frozen.

The bandit drifted near several times. Once he almost stepped on Emerick's wounded shoulder.

Drest huddled close to the young knight and tried to slow her pounding heart. Everything was strange: the shadowy woods, the man who was not her brother sleeping beside her, and hiding like that, not being out in the open, not being free. She readied herself for a night of wakefulness, yet her exhaustion and terror were so great that she sank into a dreamless sleep instead.

-← 9 →-

THE TRADE

Drest woke early, just past dawn, and for an instant didn't recognize the ferns surrounding her. Then she remembered where she was and why she had been sleeping in the woods. Forcing herself to breathe slowly, she began to stretch.

And poked the young knight in the ribs with her elbow.

Emerick recoiled, sitting up, his face yellow and sick.

"Sorry," said Drest.

He frowned and set his hand to his wound, then to his hip. "May I have my dagger back? You stole it, didn't you."

A lie came to Drest's lips. "Nay. It must have slipped out in the sea."

He seemed to weigh the likelihood. "Perhaps you'll see fit to return it when we reach the castle."

Drest struggled to her knees, careful to avoid touching him. "Can you get up on your own? We have to keep running; the bandit's here somewhere close."

Emerick sighed. "A great deal of use *I* am. A knight

should be able to defend a lass in need, even if she's the daughter of his enemy."

Drest stared. "Is that me? Am I in need? I think *you're* the one in need."

"*You're* the one being hunted by a bandit. A bandit who ate our hare, I might add. I saw him do it. He thought me little enough trouble to bother with."

"That's not a bad thing. He could have slain you."

"It's all right," said Emerick. "He didn't. You'll still have your trade." The young knight's lips twitched. "I might have thought you were concerned about my welfare just then."

"Nay, I'm concerned about finding the castle." Drest rose. "Can you get up? We should go."

He couldn't, not without help. Drest drew him to his feet.

"Come on," she muttered. "You've had a good sleep, haven't you?"

"Not as good as you; you snore like a horse."

Drest pushed down the laugh in her throat. "Uwen snores more than I do, but Wulfric—you should hear him, he sounds like a cave when the sea—"

"With any luck, I'll never have to."

Her laugh disappeared. Without another word, Drest grabbed the young knight and dragged him out of the ferns.

◄◄-►►

Drest lasted for hours before her mind became fuzzy. She wasn't sure how much longer she could stagger on with her wounded enemy through the tangle of trees and patches of sun-dappled ferns. Her last meal had been by the bonfire, nearly a day ago, and her throat and mouth were dry. At the headland, she'd have slaked her thirst by one of the forest brooks that emptied out over the stones. These woods had to have such brooks as well.

Within minutes, Drest spotted one: a shallow, muddy rush of water that flowed toward the sea. Her eyes followed the trickle and saw where it grew thick.

"We'll stop here. I need something to drink." She leaned Emerick against a tree and wandered to where the trickle had pooled.

The young knight patted his way down the trunk until he could sit. His movements were jerky, like a fish taken from the sea and set out on the beach to die. Despite herself, a swift stab of pity rushed into Drest.

"We can't argue," she said.

"Why not? That's one thing we seem to be doing well together."

She faltered. "Because—because we're on a journey."

Emerick raised a finger. "No, it's because I need you. And you need me. And that's all we must remember."

Drest dipped her cupped hands into the icy water. Flecks

of bark and dirt floated between her fingers, but she drank fully.

"It's clean water," she said, scooping a fresh cup. Tensing her fingers to leave as few gaps as possible, she carried it dripping to where the young knight sat.

He leaned toward her, but stopped with a jerk. "God's bones. I think my rib wound has opened."

"Have a drink before it all drips out and then I'll fix you."

Drest knelt beside him and put her cupped hands to his mouth.

Emerick gulped the water, then a second cup that Drest carried, then a third. When he had finished, she joined him on the ground to rest.

He looked up into the trees. "I have never slept where I could see the sky. Even on battlefields, I had a tent."

All at once, Drest remembered: She had but four days.

"I miss the castle," Emerick was saying, "even though these woods are much less smelly."

"Is your castle prison smelly?"

The knight looked at her. "Most prisons reek. Ours smells better than the rest of the castle; that's a small courtesy we pay our prisoners."

"How are they keeping my family?" Drest asked in a small voice.

"On iron rings fixed to the wall, of course." He added

quickly, "Don't think your family will escape; no one has broken free from that prison, and no one who has tried has lived. I shan't tell you more; you'd have nightmares."

Drest shuddered. "Do you think your Lord Faintree would trade my da for you?"

"I highly doubt that."

"What about this Sir Oswyn? Would he?"

"Never."

"He'll give me just one of my brothers, then? Will I really be able to choose which one?"

Emerick sighed. "I can't promise anything but the trade alone. If this lands on Oswyn's miserable head, I don't think you'll have even one of your brothers, but that will be the least of our problems."

"It sounds like you wouldn't mind something else landing on Oswyn's head. Like a boulder."

A pained laugh escaped through Emerick's lips. "For a bloodthirsty villain, you have a certain charm. Would you help me with my rib wound now?"

Drest peeled the sodden dressing from each of Emerick's wounds and washed her ripped-off tunic sleeves in the stream. She was feeling better already with the water in her belly. If they could walk quickly, they might be able to reach the castle soon. Her brothers could master any trap and her father knew a castle's ways. With luck, she'd

61

arrive at the prison and find them all waiting at the door.

"Are you cold?" asked Emerick. "I am. Perhaps you could start a fire."

Tiny bumps had risen on Drest's bare arms, but she shook her head. "Nay, we can't. It's not safe with the bandit still about. We've got to find our way out of the woods to be free of him—and to reach your castle in time."

"Oh, you'll reach it in four days. Regardless, they won't have a public execution without me." But the wounded man's face clouded. "At least they shouldn't."

It was well past midday when they emerged from the woods upon a massive dirt path that extended in both directions.

"Here's the road," Emerick said. He'd been quiet all that time and his voice was faded. "It shall lead to the castle, but it shall first lead to a village from whose good people we might beg a bite to eat."

"We can't," Drest said. "We don't have time. Do you see where the sun is?"

Emerick stopped and lifted his arm from her shoulder. "I do, but I also feel the state of my own strength. I haven't eaten, Drest, in days."

Drest walked a few more paces. The wounded man didn't move.

Emerick's silence increased Drest's anger as tinder to a fire.

She swung around and glared. "I wonder how old you are."

"I beg your pardon?"

"Have you lived for eleven years? Maybe twelve like me?"

Emerick frowned. "I have seen my sixteenth year pass and during it I held more honors than you shall ever know in your lifetime."

"Are you that old? It's funny, see, because Gobin's that old, and he's different."

"A knave rather than a knight, you mean?"

Drest waited for her new spurt of fury to settle. "Nay, my brother is a man who can bide his time. You won't hear him begging for food after a day when there's no food about. I suppose that comes natural to castle folk—weakness, I mean. That's what my da says."

"Your da can say that all he likes, but he'll soon find himself at the wrong end of a rope with the rest of his brood, and there's nothing you can do about it."

A bolt of fear shot through Drest. "You never meant to give me a trade," she managed to get out, her face hot.

Emerick said nothing.

"It was just a trick." Drest stood still. "Very well: You're out of the water and out of the woods. I'll let you go on your own now."

She turned and broke into a run.

"Wait! You need me to find the castle!"

"Nay, not anymore," she called over her shoulder. "I know this road leads to it, as you just said. And I've four days to find it."

"But the trade? It wasn't a trick; I don't mean to refuse you that."

Drest stopped and faced him again, from a distance. "You just said that my father and brothers will hang and there's nothing I can do about it. So I don't need you. And I don't want to talk to you." She turned back to the road.

"Drest? I take that back. I'll do what I can to ensure the trade, as you wish. I'm sorry. Truly. I spoke in anger."

She walked on, swinging her arms.

"Drest? Please come back."

She shook her head.

"If you go, I shall die."

Every impulse told her to take to her heels and leave him to crumple in the road.

But something stopped her.

The memory of his weight on her shoulder in the ravine.

And his face sinking under the water, stark with fear.

And his helpless form twisted in pain by the fire.

Once, Drest and Uwen had decided to battle the sea together. They had stood chest-deep in the stormy water, pounded by the swells, unmoving until a huge wave had knocked them both down. In the roiling water, they had torn each other from the sea's grasp, and staggered together back to shore. Drest had never been so glad not to be alone.

And that was how Emerick felt. She was sure of it.

Drest walked back to the wounded man and took his arm over her shoulder.

⊷ 10 ⊷

The Figure in the Field

The road was easier to walk upon than the forest floor, and they moved swiftly. Soon the sun had lowered behind the trees. It was blinding Drest on a long stretch when another unfamiliar sight lay ahead just off the road: a meadow covered by empty strips of soil.

"What's happened to that patch of land?" Drest said. "Was there a fire?"

"Have you never seen a field before?" Emerick had leaned on her more in the past few hours and straightened as they paused. "Farmers grow their crops in fields to feed themselves and their lord. But I don't suppose you'd know about farmers and their crops, what with the living flesh your family eats."

Drest stared. The wounded man had a very faint smile on his lips.

"Aye," Drest managed to get out in her old insolent tone, "that explains how knights are so weak and my family is so strong. It's the biting off live squirrels' heads that does it."

Emerick lifted his arm to stretch. The removal of his weight made Drest stumble. As she rubbed her shoulder, a shrill, hoarse caw drew her glance back to the field. Something was moving there.

A human shout—a boy's—drew Drest's attention closer. She drifted halfway down the rutted path.

A crow was hovering over a dark mound on the soil. There were six boys circling the mound, their arms raised. At first Drest thought they were holding swords, but then she recognized their weapons as sticks. Except one that was shiny at its point.

"Village boys having their fun," Emerick said, disgust in his voice. "No doubt they're hunting crows."

Drest couldn't take her eyes off the field and the boys. And the shape on the soil. She could just make it out. It was a figure swathed in a black hood. "That's a person on the ground."

Emerick stared. "God's bones, you're right. What are they doing to him? It looks—are they trying to stab him?"

It could be a maiden helpless on that field, said Thorkill's voice, thick with urgency. *Drest, lass, you must do something. Ask your friend to help.*

Drest raced to Emerick's side. "What if we went in together? I've my sword and you—we can find you a stick."

The young knight shook his head. "I can't do much with a stick, not in this condition."

"Then I'll give you my sword and I'll take the stick and—"

"I'm sorry, but I can't fight when I'm this injured, not even against village boys."

Drest cast a frantic look at the field. "Nay, but Emerick—"

"Drest, it's by the barest luck that I am standing now without your help." He sighed. "Let's go. I don't want to watch."

A shudder passed through Drest. "It's a person, Emerick. Trapped in a hood. My brothers say people get hooded only before they're executed so they can't see what's about to happen." Borawyn pressed against her leg.

Emerick took a deep breath. "There are six boys with spears, and one of those weapons is real. I can barely move, and you carry a massive sword you can't possibly expect to hold upright. Yes, someone must help, but we are not— Drest?"

She had started running before he could finish. By the time she reached the field, she had drawn her brother's sword.

✦ 11 ✦

VILLAGE BOYS

Drest sprinted across the field, the soil crumbling like ash beneath her boots. Ahead of her, the boys swung at the diving crow, while the figure on the ground lay motionless.

The boy with the real spear noticed Drest first. He shouted to his friends, pointing his weapon at her. The other boys stabbed one last time at the bird, then stepped back, uncertain of this advancing sword-wielding apparition.

The boys were not as young up close as they had seemed in the distance. Smaller than her brothers, and thin, but all were Drest's size or bigger.

Drest dashed past the retreating crow, her sword lowered, and knelt by the hooded figure on the ground. It was a boy, bound by ropes on his wrists and ankles.

"Don't worry," said Drest. "I've come to save you."

Then she stood as Gobin had taught her, her sword arm crooked at the level of her stomach, the blade steady and angled out, and rushed at the boys.

They shouted and scattered. But within an instant it

became clear that they had sized up the situation and decided that six against one gave them an advantage. Drest saw the calculation in their eyes.

You know what they're doing, don't you? Gobin's voice. *Pretending to be calm. You can do it just as well. Your confidence, lass, will unnerve the enemy. So give them your most menacing grin.*

The boys were arranging themselves in a wide circle around her. It was like the old wolf-hunting technique the twins had once described. She tried to grin as if Wulfric were standing with her, his glare passing over each boy like a spreading fire, but her face remained rigid.

The boy with the metal-tipped spear, a dirty lad her own size with blond hair even stringier than Emerick's, hissed something, and the boys raised their weapons.

You don't feel like grinning? said Gobin. *Very well. Let's strike the boy with the real spear first. Feint to one side, as if you're going at a smaller boy, then launch at him, sword low. Hold it steady, Drest, and you can complete a circle-lift.*

Gobin's voice spoke as if they were on the headland and he was guiding her sword in practice. She could almost feel his warm hands over her own.

Now!

Drest swung her sword with a low arc at the boy closest to her. He stumbled out of her way, and her uninterrupted motion lifted Borawyn's weight into the circle that started the move. She knew the technique, had practiced it so often that she needed only to guide and follow the mighty blade. As Borawyn rose, it splintered the leader's spear just a finger's length from his hand.

Now shove him, said Uwen.

Drest drove her elbow into the boy's chest and sent him sprawling to a heap on the ground.

The boy gasped, struggled, and then cried in a strangled voice, "Attack!"

A tongue of fear curled down Drest's neck.

Didn't that frighten him? murmured Gobin. *It usually frightens villagers.*

The boys fell upon her.

Drest swung madly. She chopped spear after spear, but the boys still attacked, using the sharp pieces. Drest's motions turned desperate and clumsy. A broken spear scraped the side of her head. Another poked her back and ripped her tunic.

"Are you a girl?"

The stringy-haired boy broke into the knot of boys surrounding her.

Drest's stroke was weak; they were far too close to fight with a sword. The boy ducked, and then was beside her.

"That's a girl. A *girl's* come to fight with us. Grab her!"

Before Drest could move, they had pinned her arms to her body with practiced tight grips like Uwen's.

Panic seized Drest.

What are you doing? Uwen's voice whined. *Why aren't you even trying?*

She struggled, but couldn't lift her sword.

Frighten them. Gobin's voice. *Conserve your power and lash out like a snake. Blast it, Drest, why did you not give them a menacing grin?*

A sinking, bitter fear washed over her. She had been foolish to think she could fight without one of her brothers by her side. She had failed. She would die for it, and the boy who was trembling on the furrows would die as well.

And her family. In four days.

You can't give up, lass. Nutkin's voice rang in her mind. *Remember Da's code: Accept no defeat and always fight!*

The boys were trying to force her to her knees. Drest tensed her legs, wincing at their kicks.

Why aren't you kicking back? cried Uwen. *Have you become weak and feeble like every other lass?*

A kick struck her knee, and Drest couldn't stop the whimper that escaped her lips.

The stringy-haired boy smiled.

That's not the sound to make, lass. Cry out like a wolf instead.

Wulfric's deep voice. *A battle cry to send their blood running. Reach deep down inside yourself and roar.*

A memory flashed to her mind: her eldest brother standing beside her at the headland's lookout point, showing her how to breathe, how to bellow, how to terrify an enemy by sound alone.

Drest closed her eyes and drew all her breath into her chest, then into her stomach, and then, with Wulfric's voice still in her ears, let it out in a deep, wordless roar, a voice that hardly sounded like her own.

The boys started. Three grips loosened just barely.

Enough for Drest to free her sword arm.

Lash out now, like a snake, hissed Gobin.

She dug one heel into the soil and tore herself away, giving herself enough distance to raise her sword, then swung around with Borawyn outstretched and steady.

One boy screamed, cradling his arm.

Another stumbled back, clutching his face.

The boys who were closest and might have grabbed her sword arm fell away, shrieking.

Drest put both hands over each other on Borawyn's grip. Hardly breathing, she began a full sweep. The blade sang as it flew, slicing through the air, gaining speed.

All the boys fell back, all but the stringy-haired leader,

who was frozen, his stunned eyes locked upon the blade that was even with his throat.

Drest ducked and tried to change the sword's direction, but she lost her balance. The ground seemed to rise up around her.

Borawyn caught.

The stringy-haired boy cried out, then fell on his face in the soil.

The other boys were running, some hobbling, but most in full sprints. Soon they had disappeared past the trees at the edge of the field, leaving Drest alone with the fallen boy and the hooded boy, both of whom were still.

⤙ 12 ⤚

THE LAD OF
PHEARSHAM RIDGE

A shiver shot through Drest, then a wash of cold, then the sense that she would faint. She crumpled to her knees, breathing hard, feeling only the warm soil through her hose and the biting wind on her bare arms.

It had been too quick. She hadn't been ready. She hadn't known what it would be like to slay another person.

Nay, but you had to; it's what we must do in battle. Nutkin's voice was gentle.

Breathe, my lass. Wulfric's voice.

Come on, Drest, get up. What are you doing on the soil? Are you napping or just a coward? Uwen snickered.

Shut it, snarled Gobin. *Drest, lass, you'll be all right. Take a good long breath.*

Of course she'll be all right, said Thorkill soothingly. *Breathe in, then out, then go see about that lad you saved.*

The bound figure lying in the furrows was trying to sit up.

75

Drest rose and went to him. She set Borawyn aside and with shaking hands untied his ropes.

He ripped off his hood, revealing the pale face of a boy her own age with black hair in tangles.

"I told you I'd save you," Drest said. She could not stop shaking.

The boy's gaze shifted over her face, down to her sword on the ground, then back up again. "Who are *you*?"

Drest flushed. "A mighty warrior. Like my brothers. Are you hurt?"

The boy's eyes became evasive. "Why would I be hurt?"

At first, she could not answer. "Do you not see what you hold in your hands, lad? It's a hood. It was round your whole head not long ago. Do you not know what comes to people in hoods like that?"

The boy stiffened. "Thank you for your concern, but I'm not hurt. It was just a game, and I wasn't afraid. Except when I heard those screams. Was that your doing?" He twisted around to the field, and froze at the sight of the figure lying in the soil. "Colum?"

Then the boy was on his feet, rushing to the fallen figure. He knelt beside him and murmured something, then rose swiftly.

"We must fetch help." The boy started back toward

Drest at a run. "He's not dead but he's—he's badly hurt."

Drest picked up her sword and sheathed it. "I didn't mean to hurt him."

"Is that so?" The boy stared fixedly at Borawyn. "What's that for, then?"

"Saving your life," she retorted. "Do you need to fetch help? Go on; I need to fetch my captive."

Interest flickered in the boy's face. "You have a captive?"

"I just said that, did I not? He's over there." Drest nodded toward where she had left the young knight—but saw nothing.

Your captive's like a rabbit who just got loose from a snare, sniggered Uwen's voice. *You've just lost your way into the castle.*

Drest broke into a run and heard the boy fall in behind her.

When she reached the spur that linked the field with the road, there was no sign of the wounded man—none except for an unmoving body on the path.

Emerick lay with his eyes closed, his face clenched in pain, but alive.

"I tried to help you," he said between his teeth, "fool that I am."

"What, by taking a step and falling?"

"I was attempting to join you."

"Aye, I can see. You very nearly made it a second step."
Drest knelt beside him. Two red stains shone newly wet
on his tunic. "You squirrel-headed boar's bladder. Do you
want to die on the road?"

"Does it please you to insult a man who can't move?"

"Forgive me," the boy broke in, "but Colum needs help.
I'm going to fetch our healer, and if your captive can't
move, you might want to drag him somewhere before
Colum's brother comes. He's a blacksmith with arms like
tree trunks."

"*My* arms are like tree trunks," Drest muttered. "Little
ones."

Emerick struggled to lift himself, then gave up and
rested his cheek against the ground. "What did you do out
there, Drest? I saw the boys running, and one fall. Don't
tell me you slew him."

Drest held in her shudder and nodded to the boy. "Lad,
help me lift my captive. I can't leave him here like this or
he'll trip over himself and open another wound."

The boy hesitated.

"Don't just stand there like a crushed grub," Drest said.

The boy went to Emerick's side, and together they lifted
the young knight. Drest took her place under his shoulder
once again.

◄+‑►►

The boy—his name was Tig and he was the foster son of the miller of Phearsham Ridge—led them down the road and into the woods to the healer's small stone hut. He dashed inside to tell her about Colum, then led them on, through more woods, until they came to a river flanked on both sides by a grassy meadow. Drest was surprised to see a huge wooden wheel in the water with a house upon it; she had heard of mills before, but had never seen one.

Tig led them through a door into the house. The small room into which they stepped smelled sweet, like firewood, and was filled with the creak and splash of the wheel. In the corner, a figure in a long brown tunic with a white head-cloth was staring at them.

It's your first maiden, Gobin's voice said. *That's what an ordinary maiden looks like. Long hair, smooth face. She's rather lovely, isn't she?*

"What's this, Tig?" the maiden asked in a high voice as the boy closed the door.

Tig took a deep breath. "Colum's hurt, and they—this warrior maiden and her captive—she just saved my life. So we must help her before—"

"Oh, Tig, lad, what happened?" The maiden pulled the boy into an embrace.

"Nothing. No, not nothing, but—but Colum challenged me, and so—"

"Oh, *Tig!*"

"—so we met on the fallow field, where I admit I had little advantage—"

"Did he hurt you?"

"—and I might not have come home quite whole this time. I owe this warrior—and her sword—a tremendous debt." Tig pulled away from the maiden. His face was suddenly somber. "No, he did not hurt me. Thanks to her."

The maiden bowed to Drest, holding her skirts. "I thank you with all my heart. Tig—my brother—he is not always wise in the conflicts he seeks."

"Not deliberately *unwise*, though," the boy added.

She shot him a stern look. "You know that Torold will come for you. *Again.*"

"I know." Tig glanced around the room. "So I'll hide. And could we hide them?"

"Better to have a quiet, peaceful life than *this*," muttered the maiden, then offered Drest a smile. "Where do you imagine we'd put them, Tig? I beg your pardon, miss. I do not know your name."

"My name is Drest."

"And your captive?"

"For God's sake," Emerick said. "My good maiden, I am

80

Emerick, a wounded knight from Faintree Castle. That doesn't make me a captive any more than—"

"From Faintree Castle?" The maiden's eyes narrowed. "I would not mention that here."

"Why not?" Emerick asked. "Is this not Lord Faintree's town?"

"Nay, not for years." She glanced at Tig. "The rafters? But her captive won't be able to climb."

"*Not* a captive," muttered Emerick.

The boy led them through the door in the back of the room into another space, a cavernous one. Wooden beams stretched beneath the roof from one wall to the next.

It was a massive space, empty, yet it felt enclosed and tight to Drest.

At the other end of the room, an outside door swung open and two men rushed in. Drest's fingers closed on Borawyn's grip, but she let go when she saw Tig stride across the floor.

"Father, Wyneck, a fight's coming. I'm sorry. I didn't mean—"

"Your fault?" said the older, gray-bearded man. "We saw Wimarca by the wheat field and she bade us find you quick." He set his hand on the boy's shoulder as they drew together. "What have you done, lad?"

"I—it was Colum and the other lads, and—well, I challenged them, and they went too far. But this warrior maiden rushed forth to save me." The boy paused. "That's the truth, not a story."

Frowning, the old man looked at Drest.

The younger man, as tall as Wulfric with a curly beard as wide as Thorkill's, shut the door and leaned against it. His cool gaze traveled down Drest's face to rest on Borawyn.

"You brought us dangerous visitors, my brother," he said.

Drest straightened. "Aye, we may be dangerous, but we are friends. That lad and the others—they weren't fighting fair. My da—his name is Grimbol—he always taught me that you don't fight like that and—" She stopped. "I didn't mean to slay the lad."

"Grimbol, did you say?" The old man's eyes were attentive. "So you're the daughter of the Mad Wolf of the North. His youngest?"

"Aye, I'm the youngest," said Drest. "Is that what you call my da?"

"Yes," said the older man. "He's known across the lowlands as the Mad Wolf, and feared by many."

Men's voices sounded from just outside.

"They've come!" Tig swung around and pointed at the rafters. "Climb up as fast as you can!"

Thick wooden pegs protruded in the corners of the

room where the walls met. Drest grabbed one and swung herself up. With Borawyn thumping against her leg, she scrambled up the next, then the next, until she had reached the highest post. She slid onto a beam below the roof and pulled her sword up beside her. Then she drew up her legs.

Drest had found her spot only just in time: The front door of the big room flew open.

Three broad-chested men rushed in. Wyneck and the old man turned to meet them. Drest waited to see the maiden join him—then it would be three against three—but she had shrunk to the corner, standing close to Emerick. Tig stood on his other side.

"Where is she, Arnulf?" roared the largest of the three intruders. "Where is the fiend?"

"There's no fiend here, Torold." The old man's voice was stern. "And there's no girl but Idony. Someone's told you a story."

"*There's* the witch's boy." One of the other men pointed at Tig, who flinched but otherwise didn't move.

All three started toward him.

What are you doing hiding like this when there's a fight coming? said Uwen.

"Don't think you can touch my lad," growled Arnulf as he blocked the way of the three men.

Wyneck joined him and gave Torold a fierce shove.

Do you think that old man and his son are a match for those three? You are.

With Uwen's voice ringing in her ears, Drest swung down her legs and started to inch back toward the protruding post.

But before she reached it, the mill's door opened, and the strangest figure Drest had ever seen stepped into the house.

← 13 →

THE HEALER

The figure was as tall and thin as a heron with long white hair like folded wings. A sharp nose, high cheeks, and glittering eyes made the face seem wild. The animal-skin cloak—of gray wolf, red fox, and speckled boar—added to that effect, and the skins' rank odors filled the room.

"You don't waste time, do you, Torold?" The voice, high and wrinkled, gave a bitter laugh.

It was a woman. But unlike any woman Drest could have imagined.

The men of the village cowered. Emerick and Tig did not. And neither did Drest, who met the strange woman's eyes. But the woman glanced away and showed no sign of having noticed the girl in the rafters.

"My brother lies dead upon the field," Torold said in a shaking voice. "And that witch's boy—"

"Have the other boys taken up Tig's talent for great tales?" said the woman. "Colum lies but wounded upon the field, hardly dead."

"A lass with a sword—"

"I saw no lass and no sword, just a boy in pain." The woman's eyes narrowed. "And here you stand, thirsty for revenge. It was a story, Torold, nothing more, and your brother needs you. I've done what I can, but he should not lie out in the open like that for much longer."

The large man's gaze upon the strange old woman was uneasy, but at last he strode to the door and broke into a run. His companions followed.

The old woman closed the door and stepped back into the room with a feeble, unsteady gait.

Arnulf went to her and offered his arm. "You came just in time, Wimarca."

"Yes, I figured Torold would rush to the mill. Tig, step from away from the man in blood. Come here."

The boy slipped away from Emerick and strode up to the old healer. With a twist of a smile, he waited.

Wimarca reached out and held Tig's cheek in one long-fingered hand, staring at him as intently as he stared back.

"Resentment is not a plant we should wish to cultivate," the old woman said. "Torold's shall not be easy to cut down."

"I know. That was not my intention." Tig bit his lip. "Thank you for coming."

Wimarca sniffed, but let him go and pointed at Emerick. "You look as if you could use some help."

"I would be most grateful for a healer's aid, my good woman."

"Sit by the fire, then, so I can see you clearly. And you, sword-bearing fiend in the rafters. Come down so that I may see you clearly too."

Drest scampered over the rafters and down the pegs protruding from the walls. She came down too quickly, and almost caught her scabbard on the wood. The old woman watched her with a trace of a smile.

"I never meant to slay the lad," Drest said.

"I know. You would have if you'd held to your sword's path. But you spared him. Come closer, child."

Flushing, Drest went to her. The reek of animal skins was even stronger now that she was close. Between the folds of the cloak, long strings hung around the woman's throat, beaded with sparkling bits of metal, dull gems, and one with what looked like tiny skulls.

"Mouse skulls," Wimarca said, noticing her glance. "They do wonders for a toothache." The old healer put her hand on Drest's cheek. Her fingers were dry and warm. "Thank you, child, for risking your life to save Tig's. He could use a friend such as you."

Drest twitched. "I'd be glad to be his friend, but I can't

stay. I'm on a journey to save my family, see, and my cap—my man over there, he needs healing before we set off. But we need to set off soon; Lord Faintree has my da and brothers, and he'll hang them in four days if I'm not at his castle in time."

"If you need to make haste to save the Mad Wolf and his sons, we'll help," Arnulf said.

"Tig and I will fetch supplies," Idony added.

Arnulf and Wyneck carried Emerick to the fire, and Idony and Tig disappeared through the back door. Wimarca knelt beside Emerick and took a small bag from beneath her cloak. He winced as she lifted his bloody tunic. Drest looked away.

The two men were watching her.

"You've been very good to our Tig," Arnulf said, "just as your father has been to this town."

Drest drifted over to them. "How do you mean?"

Arnulf's wrinkled face creased in a smile. "Saved our lives, he did. It was ten years ago, and this village's crops had failed. The grain rotted in every row, including Lord Faintree's demesne. I went to the castle to tell the steward, and what you do think he did? Followed me back here to take from the little we had. We'd have starved if it hadn't been for your father."

"He brought you grain?"

"No, lass: He made sure we *kept* our grain. He was passing by with his war-band—he passed by often to spend the night or have a meal—but this time he came when the castle men were here. He chased them off."

Warmth rose within Drest. "He kept them off too, did he not?"

"Yes, he did. For a month, and that was enough. No castle man who tried to take our grain left Phearsham Ridge. So they stopped coming. That demesne wasn't worth all those castle men."

Wyneck leaned close to her, his beard touching her bare arm. "Your companion speaks like a castle man," he murmured. "Are you sure you can trust him?"

"Nay, I can't, but I know that. I'm keeping him alive so I can trade him for my family."

"Take care he doesn't trick you," Wyneck said. "Castle men are funny like that."

He was about to say something else when Tig rushed back into the room, Idony at his heels.

"They're coming back!" Tig shouted. "By the river, with torches!"

The miller rose. "You should go, lass. Wyneck and I will hold them as long as we can, but you and your man had best go swiftly." He paused. "Go save your father. Every village in this land could use him."

Drest hastened to Emerick, who was pulling his tunic over the linen bandages that Wimarca had swiftly strapped around his chest. He clung to Drest's shoulder and stood.

"Go hide in the woods," Wimarca said as they started toward the door, "but take great care: As I rushed here, I saw a man on the road. Men who stand in shadows to wait and watch are often men on hunts."

Drest's mouth was dry. "That bandit. Emerick, he's followed us."

All at once, Tig was at her side, his gaze shifting between her and the young knight. "You're being followed?"

"Aye, there's a bandit after us. After me." Drest reached for her sword, trembling. "I shall have to fight him."

"Don't," said Emerick. "We've been walking all day and you're tired. He could harm you badly."

They exchanged a long, tense look, and Drest nodded. "Then we'll hide. Let's be off."

"Hold, just—just for a moment," Tig said. "I can help you. My crow and I—we can outsmart your bandit."

"Tig!" bellowed Arnulf. "Go hide before it's too late!"

"Trust me," Tig murmured. "I'll be of use to you. I swear it."

"Tig, lad!" Arnulf had thrust a rush torch into the hearth and was crossing the room with the flaming brand held high. "Did you hear what I said?"

Tig set his hands on his hips and looked up at the old man. "There is a greater purpose for me than that, Father. I must go with this maiden."

"Stop it, lad, and go hide."

"Not hide but serve," Tig said. "Think of how the Mad Wolf would see this village if I were to help his youngest child, his only daughter. He'd owe us a favor." The boy paused. "And it would keep me far from Torold. And—and this might be my quest."

Arnulf looked at Drest, then at Tig, his face stern. "*Is* this your quest? The one you always speak of?"

"It could be."

Wimarca swept in front of the miller. "A good quest for him, particularly for this time," she said, "and it would be good, Arnulf, for him to be *gone* just now."

The miller nodded, though his eyes abruptly filled with tears. "Be careful, Tig."

The boy bowed his head, then dashed forward and slipped under Emerick's free arm. Drest readjusted her grip, and together they dragged the wincing wounded man to the door. Tig did not look back, but Drest did. The miller was standing in the middle of the room, his brow furrowed, a single tear shining against his cheek in the light from his brand.

⊷⊶

In the darkness, Tig led Drest and Emerick across Phearsham Ridge's empty square to a path that joined the road. As they stepped onto the dirt, the town at their backs, Emerick stumbled and almost fell, but Drest shoved her shoulder beneath him, catching him in time.

"Wait," the young knight panted. "I can't walk this quickly. My rib wound—the healer didn't have time to tend to it, and its ache is immense."

Drest tried to listen for the bandit but heard nothing past Emerick's ragged breathing.

"We can't stop," Drest said.

A crack sounded in the woods nearby, a fallen branch breaking as if beneath a heavy step.

Tig slipped out from under Emerick's arm and stood in the middle of the road. He clicked with his tongue, and a black shape rose above him from the trees: a crow. It circled the road, cawed once, then landed heavily on the boy's outstretched arm.

"The bandit's near," Tig murmured, "around that bend. I'll trick him now. If you'll hide and keep silent, I'll lead him astray." He pointed into the woods.

"Come," Drest whispered in the young knight's ear. She was doubtful of this boy's ability to trick a bandit, but she also knew that she was too tired to battle anyone, just as Emerick had said. And if the bandit came around the bend before they disappeared in the woods, she would have no choice but to fight.

She led Emerick between the trees, walking carefully, though the young knight shuffled beside her. With each of his steps, sticks broke and leaves rustled.

"Quiet," Drest muttered.

"I'm doing my best."

Drest couldn't see clearly in the dark, yet she could smell familiar scents, and she drew Emerick toward one of rotten wood; it would be soft and would sink, not snap, at his step.

The wood gave way to a hollow where fallen leaves were thick. Drest dropped to her knees, pulling Emerick down with her.

"You were very brave rescuing Tig like that," he whispered, "but reckless. Those boys could have slain you."

"No talking," Drest whispered back, "and shut your eyes to hide them, remember?"

"Very well. Yet Drest—"

"Hush!"

Her head against Emerick's arm, Drest tried to stay alert and wait for Tig, but as the moon rose above the trees, she drifted into sleep: With her eyes shut and with Emerick's warmth beside her, as comforting as if he were one of her brothers, she couldn't help it.

⤛ 14 ⤜

THE FATE OF
THE LADY CELESTRIA

A poke on her shoulder woke Drest early the next morning. She thought first that it was Uwen and he was dangling something revolting above her face—a split-open crab or a dead bird—and she rolled over, pretending to be asleep. That motion pushed her against Emerick's side, which brought her back to the woods, and her mind flew instantly to the bandit.

She bolted up.

A black beak and a pair of black eyes set deep in black feathers was a finger's distance from her face.

Drest recoiled, and nearly knocked over Emerick, who had propped himself up behind her.

"Good morning to you, Tig," the young knight said.

The boy was sitting on a decaying log surrounded by creeping brambles. Spots of sunlight from between the leaves above him scattered at his feet. He held a sack in his lap, from which he drew three flat, round hearth breads.

The crow gave a chunk of Drest's hair a tweak; then hopped twice to land on the boy's shoulder.

"So you *don't* lash out with your sword upon waking." Tig tore a strip from one of the breads. "I wasn't sure. I sent Mordag to wake you just in case." He held the piece near his crow, who snapped it up in one bite.

"Nay, I don't lash out unless I need to." Drest yawned, and reached for a bread. It was thick and soft, much finer than the ones Drest's brothers made over the headland's bonfire. "Where's my bandit?"

Tig grinned. "Sleeping. I led him across the forest all night. He's going to wonder where he is when he wakes."

"How did you do that?"

"By listening to how you and your captive thumped about in the woods. Then I made those sounds in the opposite direction." He nodded at his crow. "We took your bandit on his own journey. Tired him out, for he fell asleep like a bairn when he stopped."

Drest took a bite from her bread. It was clean, without grit or stones, and sweet. "Did you steal this from him?"

"No, I went back to Phearsham Ridge for the supplies we'd been packing for you. Why let those go to waste?" The boy paused. "And to say a proper good-bye to Wimarca. She kindly gave me this." He fingered the warm black cloak on his shoulders, then abruptly leaned forward and set the last bread in Emerick's hand. "I beg your pardon. Here's one for you."

Emerick dropped the bread in his lap and closed his fingers on Drest's arm. With a grunt, he shifted himself back into a sitting position, facing Tig across a patch of shallow grass.

Drest looked up at the young knight beside her. "You're moving better. Do you think you can walk on your own now?"

"It's unlikely. My ribs still hurt like the devil."

Drest grinned. "My da says people call *him* the devil, but did you hear Tig's father talk about him? The Mad Wolf. I've never heard that name before."

Emerick's face clouded. "I heard that story, about Lord Faintree's men taking their grain. Phearsham Ridge doesn't need to worry about him now. The old lord has died and his son is a better man. He'd never take their grain when they needed it."

"Would he not, even if his demesne had gone bad?" said Tig. "I wasn't aware that lords could be so generous."

"They can," Emerick retorted, "if one gives them the chance."

Drest lowered her half-eaten bread. "Is the young lord the master of Faintree Castle? He's the one who set all his knights after my da, then."

"Perhaps he had a reason," Emerick said.

"He's a fish-headed swine. *That's* the reason."

Emerick reddened. "Would you like me to tell you a reason or two? Not long ago, I was chronicling the tales of your family's brutality for the castle's records."

"Da says that a man must be brutal on the battlefield if he wants to win the battle."

"Have you heard of Yettsmoor? It's a hamlet south of here, and *not* a battlefield." Emerick folded his hands in his lap. "Your brothers set fire to the huts and chased the villagers away. All because the villagers had deemed the price of your father's protection too high and refused it."

Drest's face was hot. "Someone's been telling you stories."

"Yes, the handful of people from Yettsmoor who came to the castle for help." Emerick paused. "What about Weemsdale? Have you heard that name? It's a manor hall many days west of here. A house with a farm and huts, Drest, also not a battlefield. Your brothers stole the weavings by which those villagers are known. Do you call those tributes? Was it a tribute to drag the weavers' daughters into the woods—"

"You didn't see it! My family never—"

"*I* never saw it, but many did, and they came to the castle to tell us!"

Drest was on her feet. "That's against my da's code, which says this: Honor and protect all matrons or maidens. Anyone who says my da harmed a woman is a pockmarked, worm-headed *liar!*"

Emerick's voice was hard. "That code is a mockery. Twelve years ago, he murdered a maiden: Lord Faintree's daughter. He crept into the keep, into Celestria's chamber, and—and—" He broke off and lowered his head. His lips were trembling. "Our knights rushed to her defense, but it was too late: He'd slain her, and then he slew all but one of them. Perhaps you understand now why the young Lord Faintree would like to see the Mad Wolf hanged. Lady Celestria was his sister. She was also my greatest friend."

Drest sat very still. She couldn't pretend that her family hadn't returned from war with the stolen goods that Emerick had described. And she remembered them once laughing about huts on fire, then growing quiet when they had seen her. *Nay, Drest, we're only joking. It's not fit for your tender ears.*

But the code had always been clear. Matrons and maidens were to be protected, for they were weak, her father said, and vulnerable.

"He wouldn't have hurt that lady," Drest said at last. "I know my da."

Emerick lifted his chin. "You know nothing of him."

"Have you forgotten that I've lived all my life with him?

Nay, Emerick, someone's lied to you. You can't blame my da for everything."

"Are you truly so ignorant? Can you honestly deny that your father is a vicious devil? Everyone else knows that he is."

Drest set her hand on Borawyn's pommel. "Do you think it's wise for you to talk like that?"

The young knight's eyes narrowed. "Is that how your father speaks? Will you cut me down, just as you did that village boy?"

Tig rose, his movement so sudden that the crow lifted from his shoulder.

"Please—let's have no cutting down of anyone, no more disagreements, no insults, and let's start on our way. We have only four days, do we not?"

A deep flush suffused Drest's face. "Aye, we have to keep moving, not talking."

She walked away from Emerick and straightened her sword-belt with a jerk.

Tig went to Emerick's side and helped him stand. "I've heard parts of that tragic story before, but not how the lady died. I'm sorry about what happened to your friend."

"Thank you," the young knight whispered.

Drest cleared her throat. "Which way do we go, Tig?"

"Ah. I was thinking it might be useful to stop by the village of Soggyweald on our way. They have a healer who could finish what Wimarca began with your cap—with Emerick. Then he might be able to walk on his own."

Drest drew closer. "Are you joining us for the whole journey?"

"It's my quest."

Emerick looked uncertain. "I heard your father speak of that. Tig, this isn't going to be a simple adventure. There will be danger, and no turning back."

"That's nothing new for me," said the boy with a ghostly smile. "My foster father knows that I am destined for danger, adventure, and great things—or that's what I've been telling him."

Emerick's expression did not change. "Are you willing to risk your life for two people you don't know? You're not bound to any promise."

"I should be glad to be bound to a legend such as hers." Tig gave Drest a little bow. "And I'm not afraid."

Drest frowned. "You may not be afraid in the sun in these woods, but we don't know what will happen when we reach the castle. Are you sure, lad?"

"I've never been this sure of anything. And as I said before, Mordag and I will be of great service to you both. Now please, accept my help, or I'll just trail behind you the whole way."

Drest bit back her smile. "Come with us, then." She patted Borawyn's hilt. "And I'll protect you."

"I'll protect you as well." The boy pretended to draw a sword from his belt and stagger beneath its weight. "In my own way. Even though *you're* the legend."

Then he took his spot again beneath Emerick's arm.

Mordag flew up under the highest branches above their heads. Drest began to follow the crow, but Tig called her back.

"I'm not as strong as you," said the boy.

As Drest slipped under Emerick's other arm, she wondered: *Was* she truly strong? Strong enough to rescue her family from Faintree Castle without their help? Compared to them, she was but a wee lass, and a wee lass could never do such a thing.

But Tig had called her a *legend*. And a legend could do anything.

⊷ 15 ⊷

SOGGYWEALD

The path to Soggyweald was no path at all. The three travelers pushed through bushes and ducked under branches until they came upon a faintly trodden deer run. Soon after, the trail became wet.

"It's like pottage after the tenth day," Drest said. Her father had often made a pot of it with old dried peas and slivers of smoked fish for flavor. Day after day, she and her brothers would add fresh water to extend their meal. "Pottage with wild greens that stick to your throat."

"Pottage with a pebble," Tig said. "That's the way Idony makes it, always with a pebble she's missed. You never know when you'll break a tooth."

"I've never eaten pottage." Emerick's boot slid on the mud. "Nor do I wish to if it looks like this."

"It's better than shore mud," said Drest. To Emerick's shocked look, she added, "Which I do *not* eat."

"Or grains-and-dung," said Tig with a smirk.

"Don't tell me the people of Phearsham Ridge eat *that*," said Emerick.

"No, but once when the farmers were spreading the fields, I picked up a handful and slipped it in Colum's pottage. He never noticed. I was sure he would."

The path turned into liquid mud, and the leaves and clustered tree roots that covered it were slick.

The first time Drest slipped, she stranded Emerick in a puddle, ankle-deep. The second time, he sprawled into the muck, his face a mask of pain. And once Tig sunk up to his knee in a swirl of mud and water. He withdrew his leg with a shake and a shrug.

"Refreshing," the boy said, and quickly resumed his spot beneath the wounded man.

"Is this Soggyweald, then?" groaned Emerick.

"Have courage," said Tig. "We're nearly at the shore."

At last, after creeping and slipping for hours, they were through. The ground became abruptly dry, and they saw before them a pair of wooden posts that marked the village. Just past, a stone hut stood with a series of short wooden stumps against its wall. Beyond it stretched a line of smaller huts.

"Soggyweald congratulates you for surviving," said Tig. With Mordag on his shoulder, he held out his arm, encompassing the village. "And that"—he nodded at the stone hut—"is the healer's home."

Gasping, Emerick slid onto a stump.

"I'll fetch her." Drest walked around the hut slowly, taking care where she stepped. Woven sticks formed a wet, glistening path.

The door was open. She stole inside.

The reek of dead plants almost choked her. Drest sank to her knees, a cough echoing through her chest. Yellow dust was drifting down over her head. She crawled away, out of its path, and watched it spill in a slow stream from a basket at the top of the door. The back of her neck itched madly where the dust had fallen.

"Is anyone here?" Drest shook the dust out of her hair and struggled to her knees.

The hut seemed larger than it had from the outside. Pale brown weavings with patterns like the lines of the paths in the headland covered the stone walls. Clay bowls and jars, small rush baskets, and sheaths of herbs wound up in string were scattered on a table by a shuttered window. Halfway across the room, a circle of black ashes marked where the healer kept her fire. Past it, near the wall, a rope ladder led to an alcove in which Drest could just see the trailing edge of a cloak.

"Are you the healer?" Drest tried to stand, but nausea pulled her back to the floor, and she lay there gasping. "Your dust—it's made me sick."

No one answered.

Drest closed her eyes and focused on breathing. It was almost as if she were underwater in a placid cove with tendrils of sea plants winding around her ankles, holding her, pulling her, tightening—

She sat up, her heartbeat throbbing in her ears.

"Where's the healer?" Drest muttered, and forced herself to rise.

Now that she was standing, she saw the hut clearly. The patterns in the weavings were just shadows and folds, nothing more. The bowls and herbs on the table had been shoved aside. And the cloak in the alcove—it was only a blanket.

The hut was empty.

A faint noise came from outside. It took her several moments to realize that Emerick was calling her name.

"Drest?" His voice was distant. "Lass, can you hear me?"

Her head began to throb. Staggering back, she carefully stepped over the spilled dust and darted outside.

A burst of fresh air cleared her head, leaving only a lingering ache. As Drest took her first step on the slippery woven path, she noticed print in the dirt close to the hut. It was cloven, like that of a deer, and recent. It had not been there when she had entered.

A movement in the corner of her eye made Drest look up. She caught a glimpse of antlers as a huge tawny creature lumbered into the woods. A stag. It was almost as if the beast had been outside watching while she had been within.

Drest hastened back to her companions.

"We've been calling you." Emerick reached out, and Drest stepped under his arm. "We heard you enter but then nothing, not for many minutes."

"I was looking for the healer. That hut—it was strange." Drest didn't want to mention the dust, which was now burning on her neck, or the stag.

"All the huts are strange," said Emerick. "We could see no movement in any of them."

Tig stood next to him, frowning. His crow hunched low against his hair and cheek.

"Let's look for the healer," said Drest. "Or someone who can tell us where she is."

Holding Emerick steady, Drest started on the path that led between the huts.

They had walked only a few steps when a raucous cheer rose from deep in the town. It made Drest think of the war cries that Wulfric had taught her.

"A celebration?" Emerick did not sound confident.

Drest led the way, her senses alert. Something about this town was wrong, yet nothing seemed to be out of place. Each hut was made of logs and sticks and topped with tight thatch. Lavish blossoms of white and blue billowed in gardens; others were planted with tender green vines. For a village stuck within a bog, it was surprisingly tidy.

Yet Tig's eyes narrowed and he cast every house a suspicious look.

The path turned, and Drest found herself facing the back of a large crowd.

Gobin had once told her about the time that he and Nutkin, scouting ahead for the war-band, had run into a mob of villagers. It was the only time he'd been afraid.

"Do you smell that?" said Emerick. "There's a bonfire ahead." He staggered forward, dragging Drest, and tapped on the shoulder of a small figure who stood a little apart from the crowd, a fair braid down her back. "I beg your pardon, but what is this celebration?"

The maiden looked over her shoulder. She was barely older than Drest and wore the same kind of long brown tunic as Idony.

"We're burning our witch," she said. "Have you not heard? She's been found guilty of all the charges."

Drest was very still. Grimbol had told stories at the headland of how such things came to pass, and how important it was to stop them.

Emerick frowned. "This is a village of Lord Faintree, is it not? He would not take kindly to the burning of any person."

The maiden shook her head. "It doesn't matter; he'll never know." She added in a low voice, "But keep quiet if you don't want the village on you." It was as much of a threat as a warning.

Emerick's face hardened, but he said nothing further to the maiden, who went back to the spectacle.

"We shouldn't stand here," murmured Tig.

"Nay," said Drest, an idea beginning to grow in her mind. "We've work to do."

Quickly, pulling Emerick along with her, Drest skirted the crowd and returned to the main path. She led them out to the top of a low hill where they could see the village square below.

The mob filled it, up to a narrow platform with a huge wooden post where a woman in white was bound. Her long hair—silver, it seemed, for it sparkled in the midday light—was loose upon the wind. Beside her stood a man with a staff who was shouting to the crowd. Another man stood at the foot of the platform, holding a torch aloft.

Go down there, Drest, or that woman will die, murmured Thorkill's voice.

Honor and protect all matrons and maidens, said Gobin. *Don't forget the code.*

Nutkin's voice added, *I know you didn't, lass, but you need to show it now.*

If I were beside you, said Wulfric, *I'd teach these villagers what happens when they harm a woman.*

If I were beside you, said Uwen, *we'd make a thousand wee pieces out of all those pig-spotted rat innards.*

Drest disengaged herself from Emerick's arm. "Tig, take care of Emerick for me. Take him somewhere safe, and hide. I'll catch up with you in the woods."

"What are you doing?" Emerick grabbed for her, but she skipped out of his reach. "Drest, wait! You haven't the strength to challenge a mob!"

"They won't touch me if I'm quick. Take him, Tig!"

A look of fear and awe flashed in the boy's face, and he slipped into Drest's spot under Emerick's arm.

"Drest, come back!" Emerick shouted.

But Drest had already dashed down the path toward the mob.

⊰ 16 ⊱

MEREWEN

The mob roared.

Drest pounded into it, her feet racing nearly as fast as her heart. There was no clear path between people, but Drest shoved against the first wall of bodies, her fingers fixed around Borawyn's grip.

"Someone's never seen a burning before." A man as craggy and narrow as a tree chuckled as Drest pushed past him. "Slow down, lad. We're reading the charges. There are still a few left."

"I need to reach the front," snarled Drest.

Other villagers, hearing their words, glanced back and smiled. And to Drest's astonishment, they moved aside to make room.

"Are you a stranger to this town?" a woman asked. "Come to see a fine sight? I promise you won't forget this one, lad."

"Neither will you," Drest returned.

A girl she pushed past saw the sword on Drest's hip, and stared, blushing.

"Ah, we've a young warrior among us," said an old man, and gave Drest his place.

Soon Drest was at the front.

The man with the staff was in the middle of a long recitation about evil spells, snakes, and ravens, but Drest suspected he was almost done: The man with the torch was inching closer to the platform, nodding to himself as if rehearsing in his mind.

Drest looked up and met the witch's eyes—gray eyes in a strangely young face that was marked with scars. For an instant, staring at those eyes, Drest's heart froze. Then she slipped her sword from its scabbard and stepped out of the crowd.

The man with the torch saw her first and laughed. "No, no, lad, it's my job, not yours."

He was still laughing as she darted past him, but he stopped when she scrambled up onto the platform.

"Lad!" he called. "Get down from there! Do you want her to cast a spell on you?"

The witch did not take her gaze from Drest. Close up, her eyes were like a falcon's: sharp and impassive. She looked nothing like Wimarca. Unlike Tig's healer, this one was truly wild.

"Don't move," Drest said.

It took only one swing to cut the witch's ropes—

Borawyn sang richly on the post—and then another to knock the torch out of its bearer's hands. The bark and twigs at his feet immediately crackled into flame.

Well done, lass, said Wulfric's voice. *Now shout at them. Give them a warning.*

Drest swung around to face the crowd. "Stand back unless you wish to meet my sword!"

"You stand back too," the witch murmured, "and follow me, unless you want to get caught."

The man's staff swung down close enough to nearly strike Drest's sword-hand. She turned and jumped after the witch's billowing white shift.

"This way," said the witch, taking a narrow path between huts.

Drest raced after her. The path opened up to a field high with young green plants that bent but did not break under their steps as they rushed through.

The witch plunged into a thicket of trees. Branches scratched Drest's bare arms, but she didn't slow. Her heart was pounding almost to the point of bursting. She'd done it. She'd rescued the witch. She'd obeyed her father's most important code. It was like one of his stories.

The witch stopped short and pulled Drest down in a hollow near a tree. She drew a broad, leaf-covered branch over them and crouched there.

"Don't say a word," she panted.

Drest stared at the witch's face. The silvery gray eyes were frantic yet fierce, like the fox that Drest and Uwen had once cornered in the ravine. Faint old scars patterned her skin, as plentiful as the ones that lined Grimbol's face, but a few were the red of recent wounds.

"I don't know who you are, but I owe you my life." The witch seemed about to say something else, but the villagers' voices were louder.

Drest held her breath, her fingers damp on Borawyn's grip.

The villagers never came upon them. Soon their shouts were far away. Then everything was silent but for the wind rustling in the trees.

The witch threw back the branch. Breathing hard, she tried to rise, but sank to her knees instead.

"That was nearly too much for me. I must be getting old and weak."

Drest sat up. "Do you think you're weak? You just escaped an angry mob."

The witch gave her a faint smile. "In my youth, I would have slain them all. I didn't even think of it this time." She rose to her feet.

Drest remembered Emerick and the rib wound that Wimarca had not tended.

"Are you the village healer?" Drest asked.

The witch laughed: a low, dry sound. "Would they do *that* to a mere healer? No, I'm their witch. Though yesterday I was their healer."

Drest clambered to her feet. "Why would they do that? What's wrong with this village?"

"Every village is the same. A word of advice: If you know you cannot save a family from a fever, don't even try. Murder them outright, then flee before anyone can burn you."

Drest backed away. She was no longer eager to ask this healer for anything, even if Tig trusted her.

The witch noticed her movement. Bitterness flared in her eyes. "You fear me?"

Drest straightened. "I don't fear anyone. But you sound like a madwoman, and I don't want your help."

A low laugh. "Have I offered any?"

"Nay, and I was going to ask, but I don't want it now." Drest started to turn away.

"Wait."

The witch's hand flew to Drest's shoulder and gripped tight. Drest ducked beneath it, and twisted. If she had not wrestled so often with her brothers, she would have remained caught, but with that twist she was free—and two steps away, her sword ready.

"Don't touch me," she said.

The witch started, and pointed at Borawyn's hilt. "Where did you get that sword?"

"It's my brother's. He left it for me." An ache like a bruise had begun to emanate from the place on her shoulder where the witch had grabbed. Drest raised her chin. If she could, she'd make this wild woman afraid of *her*. "We're part of the Mad Wolf's war-band, see. Have you heard of us? We're led by a bloodthirsty warrior named Grimbol. I'm his daughter."

The witch's eyes fixed on her, unmoving, just like a hawk's. "What is your name?"

"Drest." She thought of what Emerick had once said. "Like the savage Pict."

"Drest." A whisper. A breath.

Then the witch shook her head. "Put away that sword. I shan't hurt you. I shan't frighten you again, I promise." A strange expression—half smile, half grimace—came to her face. "That *you* should be the one to save me is—is rather extraordinary."

Drest lowered Borawyn. "Have you heard of me? Has my legend already traveled here? In a day?"

"I know your legend well," said the witch slowly. "I knew your father. But I never expected to see *you* here." She shook her head again. "You said you needed help. What do you need? If I can, I'll give it to you."

Drest slid Borawyn back into its scabbard. "I've a wounded knight traveling with me, and he needs a healer. I can't let him die, see, because my da and my brothers are being held in Faintree Castle, and the lord will take this knight for them."

"I haven't my salves and tinctures on me," said the witch, "but I'll do what I can. Where is this knight?"

"Hiding in the woods at the other end of the village."

"Show me."

They found Emerick leaning against a tree, a short distance from the village, and Tig on the path before him, his crow on his shoulder.

"You were supposed to hide!" Drest ran up to Tig and struck him lightly. He pretended to stagger.

"We *were* hiding. I just spotted you." Tig turned to the witch and gave a low bow.

"You, Tig," murmured the witch, "I did not expect to find you here, either. Did you bring her to me? How did you know?"

"How did I know? Do you mean what state you'd be in? I had no idea that we'd find you tied to a stake; I'd thought we'd find you in your hut, and you would be able to help this knight—"

"No matter!" The witch's voice was agitated. "Come here, Tig. I always tell you a tale when you visit. I've a new one for you, and I'll whisper it quick. It's about what healers should do to faithless villages."

Drest edged away and strode over to the young knight. "Da's code: Don't let anyone hurt a woman. Even a witch. She's the healer too, and she's going to help you."

Emerick's jaw was taut. "You could have been slain."

"I've not been slain and I saved her, Emerick. Just me, against a whole village. Tell *that* to anyone who doesn't think that a lass can fight and win."

Emerick's hard expression changed to horror. "For God's sake, Drest, don't tell me you risked your life to prove that point!"

He was about to say more, but the witch approached. "Are you the knight? You look more like a washed-up magpie. Where are you hurt?"

Emerick snorted, but then he raised a corner of his tunic to reveal the bloody bandage around his ribs.

The witch winced. "I can't help with that. I haven't healed battle wounds in years, and *that*—I would need yarrow, thornapple, and agrimony. And I have nothing." Her eyes traveled up and down Emerick's figure. "But you, my friend, you're young and strong. I've no doubt that you'll reach the castle alive."

"Aye, he's managed," Drest said, "but he's in awful pain."

A cruel smile flashed on the witch's face. "Everyone deserves a little pain. Especially a knight from Faintree Castle." She turned to Drest. The smile faded. "I'm sorry. I would help you if I could."

"If you won't help him," Drest muttered, "I'd like to see you give a wee bit of pain to the bandit who's following me. But I'd rather you help Emerick."

"A bandit's following you?"

From Tig's shoulder, Mordag gave a harsh *creea*.

"Someone's coming." Tig squinted down the path, then pointed. "I see torches."

With a low curse, the witch rushed up to the woods and pushed through a cluster of young alders to reveal a narrow opening between the trees behind. "All of you, go down this path. No one will see you on it. Go as fast as you can."

Grumbling under her breath, Drest marched to the parting between the trees, but stopped when she had stepped past it.

"I just saved your life. You owe me something. I'll come back one day and ask for it, but what's your name? So I can find you."

The witch's eyes narrowed. "You saved my life and you may take my name for it. It's Merewen. Now be gone!"

Merewen. Something about that name called to a memory in Drest's mind. But all was foggy, and Tig was already on the path, and Emerick was tugging at her.

"Come with us, Merewen!" Tig called. "Forget that talk about faithless villagers!"

The witch shook her head. "I cannot forget, not after what they've done. *They* shall not forget, either."

The young alders swished back into place.

"What's she about to do?" said Drest. "Do I need to save her life again?"

Pulling at Emerick, Tig dragged them both on. "She's going to try to burn the village—and it's better if we just go now."

"Is she mad? They just tried to burn *her*—"

"Hurry!"

Tig let Emerick go and started off at a run down the path ahead of them. Drest had to grab the young knight by herself to follow.

Her heart was pounding with anger. She wished she had room to run, to fly down the path as she had sprinted on the headland. But she couldn't, not with Emerick's weight upon her shoulder. And so Drest focused on her steps, counting them to calm down. After the twenty-fifth, she glanced back.

Trees and nothing else, not even a trace of the path, stood behind them, as if the growth had sprung up at their feet as they had walked.

Dark clouds swept in, shadowing the path. Tig continued to lead, his pace swift.

"I know we had to flee the villagers," Drest grumbled, "but that witch owed me more than her name."

"You're very lucky," Tig said over his shoulder. "A witch like her—and indeed, that's what she is—doesn't take kindly to demands. You shouldn't have spoken to her like that."

"Why? Am I not as good as she?"

"Yes, of course you are, but there are people in this world, Drest, who don't follow the basic tenets of human kindness. It's best not to cross them."

"I only asked for help." Drest sighed. "We have four days, and we wasted half of one to go to Soggyweald and save her life."

"Tig," said Emerick, "do you know how close we are to Launceford?"

"Is that the nearest town to Faintree Castle? The market town? I was there once, but by horse. By foot from here—two days, perhaps?"

They trudged on in silence. Clouds hid the sun. All at

once, Drest wanted to be out of the woods and on the road.

She glanced back again. The trees and bushes that had sprung up behind them seemed as dense and real as ever. But she noticed something strange: The path was turning. They were subtle turns, but each new turn hid the one behind it.

And then she smelled it: a faint whiff of smoke. But it was not like the smoke that rose from the bonfire on the headland. This smoke was bitter with an undercurrent of mud—a smell like burning thatch.

⊰ 17 ⊱

THE WITCH'S SON

At last, they emerged from Merewen's secret path onto the road. Though she was in the open air again, Drest was tense, as if she could still feel the witch's grip on her shoulder. She was certain that they had barely drawn ahead of Phearsham Ridge. The delay in Soggyweald had been for nothing.

Nay, not nothing, murmured Thorkill's voice. *You saved a woman, after all.*

A horrible woman, thought Drest. *The code shouldn't exist for women like her.*

They walked on past groves of ash and aspen, then bogs and dead trees, then more living woods. Drest's mood grew ever bleaker, as if with the sky, which became dark from a brewing storm that never broke. Doggedly, Drest kept on, her footsteps pounding a rhythm: *four days, four days, four days.* When Emerick stumbled and lifted his arm, she realized that her entire back was damp with sweat.

"May we stop and eat?" Emerick said. "We've walked since dawn."

"We haven't time to stop," muttered Drest, but her mouth was dry and her throat felt hollow.

They stopped on the side of the road and Tig handed around two more hearth breads, two dried trout, and a clay flask of sweet ale. The bread wasn't as soft as it had been before and the fish was too salty, but Drest bolted down both.

"And *that*," said Tig when they were done, "is the last of our food. I'm sorry we packed so little; I told Idony we'd get more in Soggyweald."

Emerick lay down on the road. "I wish you'd said that before; we could have saved some."

"We all needed it," Tig said gently, "perhaps more than you think."

Drest stood over the young knight's outstretched figure. "Don't fall asleep. We've only three days after today."

And at those words, she felt sick.

Drest wandered aimlessly toward the bend in the road. The landscape was starting to change. Ahead of her, everything looked bare: The woods were thin and the land around them empty and green but for copses of oaks. The air was stagnant and thick.

Drest closed her eyes. If only those fields were the sea. The smell of brine and wet stones, the crisp whip of the shore wind—she longed for them as with a whole new thirst.

Tig drifted to her side, his crow on his arm. "That was very brave, what you did for Merewen. I've heard many stories of witches burned at the stake, but never one that ended with a rescue. You really *are* a legend."

Drest looked up and shrugged. "My da and brothers are all legends; I'm no different from them." For the first time, it was true; she had just proved it.

But Tig's next words doused that feeling: "Oh, *you're* different. I've heard the legends of your family, and they're not like what yours is going to be." He gave a short laugh. "They're like what Merewen is known for."

"What's she known for? I've never heard of her."

"You wouldn't have. Only other witches know *her* legends, and they keep them quiet."

"How do *you* know her legends, then?"

Tig's eyes sparkled. "What if I told you that I might be a witch myself? That my mother was a witch, that I know the ways of witches and their stories and need only a *quest* to make my own?"

On his shoulder, Mordag gave a grumbling *creea*.

"I only know about sea witches, and they're really only seals." But Drest didn't take her eyes off the boy. "Is what you said true, or are you mocking me?"

Tig's grin disappeared. "I'd never mock you. I'd mock the people who mocked you. I'd mock them to misery. No, Drest, I was just telling you what I am."

She didn't know what to say. She looked up into the cloudy sky, where a layer of mist hung above the world.

"You're not at all curious?"

Drest looked back at the boy. "I don't know what to think of it. Should I be afraid of you? I was afraid of Merewen." She could admit that now, out on the road.

Tig shook his head. "What's the difference between a witch and a warrior? Or a knight, for that matter. None. We're all the same, if you take away our trappings."

"Birth; that's the difference. I was born a warrior, see."

"You were born a maiden, but you're not like Idony, nor the lady in Emerick's story."

"Aye, but I was born a warrior too. That part—my da's part—is stronger in me. It's like Emerick—he was born to be a knight, but he's not like a knight, is he? Something else is strong in him."

"You're very good to him," Tig said softly. "He is your enemy, is he not?"

"Of course I'm good to him," Drest said. "I can't have him die, can I? Besides, we can't be enemies, not when we're traveling together like this. Later, maybe, but I hope not." She glanced over at the young knight lying on the road a short distance from them. "I know I'm not supposed to, but I like him."

"So do I."

They stood together, watching Emerick's chest rise and fall, the afternoon heavy and warm around them.

"Where's your mother?" Drest suddenly turned to Tig. "You just said she's a witch. If that's true, then she must be a healer, and she could help me keep Emerick alive by fixing that rib wound. Is she on our way?"

Tig snorted. "No, she isn't, and no, she can't help us. She's dead."

"She wasn't—she wasn't burned, was she?"

Mordag leaned over and nuzzled against Tig's jaw. Absently, he stroked her head.

"No, our village hanged her."

A shock passed down Drest's spine, as distinct as a finger of ice.

"Did you go after them?" she managed to get out.

"I was but six years old, Drest." He paused, then went on coolly, "She was a healer. They did to her what most towns do when a healer fails."

"How does a healer fail?"

"Don't you know? My mother always said she was lucky; she never had to care for anyone who was truly ill. Until one old woman was, and died, and her husband never forgave my mother. *That's* how a healer fails."

Softly, he told her more: of other illnesses, other deaths.

Then one day, Otto the brewer, who had always been a friend, bound Tig to a staff and thrust it in a hole in the middle of the town square. His young son had become ill with fever. So Otto went to Elinor, Tig's mother, and told her that if she did not save his son, he would hang hers. Elinor insisted they free Tig, or she would never heal anyone again. Otto refused. His boy died that night. The villagers hanged Elinor at dawn. Despite Otto's threat, no one could bear to hang Tig. They took him deep into the woods and abandoned him instead. It was winter, and he would have died if Wimarca had not found him the next day and brought him back to Phearsham Ridge.

The boy was silent, his face grim.

"What's your village called?" Drest asked. "And where is it?"

"Why do you want to know? For vengeance? You'd be too late; Caervaerglom is empty now."

"You've been back?"

"No," Tig said quickly. "Wimarca and Arnulf went. To see if they had a new healer, and to warn her. But no one was left in the town when they got there. Everyone had died from fever, or fled. Too bad they gave up my mother; she could have healed at least *some* of them."

Abruptly, the boy stopped.

"There, a mirthful story to round out our day. We

should be off if you don't want to waste more time. We don't want all *your* family to die too."

Drest flinched, pricked by Tig's tone, then stomped over to the young knight.

"Get up, Emerick. I'm sorry, but we've got to go."

The young knight sighed. "We have three days."

"Aye, only three. Come on. Give me your arm."

He grumbled, and was too stiff to rise without help from both Tig and Drest, but at last they had him on his feet.

"We can stop again at the next town—but for food, not sleep," Drest said. "Tig, can you do that?"

The boy nodded. "I can walk all night."

"I can't," groaned Emerick. "I can barely walk as it is."

"I know you can walk. Your wounds are hardly oozing. Come on, Emerick. Show me what a knight can do, or we'll think you're less than a wee lass from the headland."

Emerick cast her an icy look. "Do you think a challenge like that will work?"

"Nay, but I thought I'd try. Come on, you maggot-headed squid. Start walking, you craven mass of muddy hose."

"Has it ever occurred to you to speak sweetly to get your way?"

"Nay. Are you ready?"

Emerick sighed and adjusted his grip on her shoulder.

Their pace had only begun to smooth out when Mordag rose from Tig's arm and shot above the road, disappearing around the bend. Tig abruptly stopped.

"What is it?" Drest said.

The road was silent. Woods had crowded both sides again, and the trees were silent too.

Suddenly, Mordag's caw echoed through the growing dark.

"It's your bandit." Tig frowned. "When she calls like that—it means an enemy is near."

Drest set her hand on Borawyn's wide pommel.

Nay, lass, murmured Gobin's voice. *This is no time to wield your sword.*

You'd better hide, said Nutkin. *Be like the barnacle, just as Da said.*

A sudden despair swamped Drest. It was as if the whole world had been slain around them—all the villagers of Soggyweald, Tig's mother, and her father and brothers too, and only the three of them on the road and the bandit were left.

The boy raised his eyes to Drest's and gazed at her intently, as if he could see her thoughts.

"You'll get to your family in time," Tig said. "That's why I'm here, isn't it? Now go on, and let me be useful."

⭆ 18 ⭆

THE STORY OF THE MAD WOLF

Drest watched Tig slip out from under Emerick's arm and start toward the bend. Mordag was flying back.

"Be careful," called Emerick.

"Go on," said the boy without turning around, holding out his arm for Mordag to land. "I'll find you when I'm done."

Done doing what? A terrible foreboding pricked at Drest, and at that moment, more than anything, she didn't want to see Tig walk around that bend.

But he did, and was gone, and Emerick was pulling her back along their path.

Night fell as they walked. Drest took as much of Emerick's weight as she could to help him swing along. Her back was soon hot and damp against the chill.

"I'm sorry I haven't let you rest, but if we keep on, I know we'll reach my da," Drest said at last. They had walked a long stretch in the dark without speaking. She had been thinking of Tig, and wondering where he was.

"Your da," Emerick murmured. "It's still strange for me to hear Grimbol spoken of as anyone's da." He glanced at Drest and then was silent, as if weighing what he was about to say. "Did you know that your father once served in the old Lord Faintree's army?"

Drest almost stumbled. "I know he fought alongside knights, but he never said whose. Are you sure?"

"He was a famous man-at-arms, known to show great strength and courage in battle. Grimbol the Savage, they called him."

"That's it; that's my da." That explained why Wulfric's old shield bore the castle's tree. "Why did Da leave the army? He never told us."

"The old Lord Faintree had one story," Emerick said slowly. "Your father disappeared in the middle of a battle, then went to the old lord when all the fighting was over with a story of having lain wounded. The old lord said it was a lie, that Grimbol had abandoned the field, and shunned him. Your father stayed with the army on the march to the castle, but when they reached it, the old lord turned him away for cowardice."

Drest was quiet. None of that sounded like her father: from being wounded to being called a coward.

"But other knights told another story: that Grimbol *had* been gravely wounded and was lucky to have lived. He'd taken a fierce blow to save Sir Oswyn, my uncle, and had lain for several hours unconscious while the battle raged around him. When he woke, the battle was done. That he'd served with honor—*he* knew that as well as anyone. So he staggered to the old lord's tent, expecting not only balm for his wounds but praise for his bravery and the important life he'd saved, but instead received the old lord's scorn. The rest of the story is the same."

"Was Sir Oswyn his battle-mate? A rotten battle-mate if he didn't help my da when he needed it." Drest shook her head. "And why did the old Lord Faintree do that? Did you not just say my da was a good warrior?"

"I've wondered why. All I can think is that perhaps Grimbol was *too* good. Perhaps the old lord feared his strength. Perhaps he suspected that Grimbol was more faithful to another man—to Oswyn—and would stand for Oswyn if he ever wished to challenge the old lord. There, I've told something good about your father."

Drest listened to the rhythm of their step. "Did you fight in that battle?"

"That was many years ago. I was but a child."

"Did you ever meet my da?"

Emerick waited before answering. "When I was small."

"Did you fight him?"

"Unlike you, I don't rush blindly into battle when I haven't a chance. No, I gave him an apple."

Drest laughed. "Did you really?"

"Celestria told me to. She was afraid she'd be beaten if she did it herself; she was not to talk with the men-at-arms, and certainly not Grimbol. She was thirteen then, nine years my senior, and I obeyed her every wish."

Drest looked up at Emerick. A strange gentleness had crept over his face.

"I was terrified of Grimbol; we had all heard stories of him. I was shaking as I handed him the apple and recited Celestria's words."

"What did he do?"

Emerick was quiet. "He knelt beside me and asked if I wanted to share it."

Drest grinned. "Was it a good apple?"

"I don't know; I was far too scared to take the half he cut for me."

"You should have."

Emerick did not return her smile. "Celestria loved Grimbol. She would haunt the places where he might go and they would talk together in corners of the bailey by the wall. I sometimes followed them. When the old lord refused Grimbol and sent him away, Celestria was sick with grief. For months, she sent word for him to return, sent it with every merchant, bard, pilgrim, and beggar who came to the castle, praying her messages would reach him. For months, she was all but mad." Emerick's voice had grown thick. "That he could murder a lass who loved him so dearly, all for revenge against her father, showed us the truth: that he was savage throughout, a true wolf in human form."

Drest stopped walking. "If she loved him, he'd never hurt her. It's not just the code, but the way my da is. Someone's lied to you, like I said."

Emerick's face was damp with exhaustion and emotion. "Sir Maldred would never lie; he was the one knight who escaped your father, the one knight who went to Celestria's defense and lived."

"He must have lied," Drest insisted. "Or someone else murdered her and ran off without your Sir Maldred seeing him."

"Ran off the cliffs into the raging sea? That's what Grimbol did. Who else do you know who can swim like your father?"

"Even my da can't swim in a raging sea! There had to be a boat, and someone else—"

"How can you keep denying it? Your father murdered a young maiden. Perhaps his code came after, out of guilt, but he was a monster then."

They stood apart in the middle of the road, breathing hard. Emerick was slumping, but she wasn't about to help him.

Suddenly, a clatter came up the road behind them: the sound of running boots.

It was Tig, pale-faced and panting, a shadowy figure in the darkness. As he drew close, Drest saw that his cloak was gone and the collar of his tunic was torn.

Mordag—a sound of wings and a shape in the sky—flew above his head, then swooped over the trees and landed on a branch not far from the road.

"I'm sorry," Tig gasped. "I've failed. And now we have to hide."

⊰⊱ 19 ⊰⊱

THE STAG

Drest and Tig took their places beneath Emerick's arms, and the three lurched across the empty road and crashed into the woods. They made no attempt to conceal the sounds of their steps.

"Here!" Tig drew up short beside an ancient pine with branches that seemed to reach beyond the midnight sky.

"Must we climb that?" Emerick moaned.

Tig pointed to a fallen branch as wide as a cloak, strewn with moss. Struggling, he tried to lift it. "Help me, Drest!"

She let Emerick go and with both hands lifted the front of the branch, tearing up a hollow in the soil.

"There," Drest said. "Both of you, crawl in. Quick."

Emerick sank to the ground and slid under the branch with a groan. Tig climbed after him, leaving space for Drest. She crawled between them and lowered the branch to rest against her shoulders. A second later, Mordag's caw exploded above them.

A footstep creaked on the twigs close by. There was quiet, then the sound of boots scraping bark: The bandit was climbing the tree. Those sounds became distant, but grew louder as he returned. His steps circled, and again he stopped before the hollow where they hid.

"Come on, girl, I'm tired of this. Come out and let's have a talk. You owe me that much. Ask your father why."

Ask Da? Drest thought. Grimbol had always spoken harshly of bandits, called them worthless rats with no sense of loyalty. Drest shuddered to think of what he must have done for the bandit to go to such pains to hunt her.

A whimper came up from Drest's throat, and she could not fully stifle it.

Quiet, lass, whispered Thorkill's voice in her mind. *Stay calm. He won't see you if you're silent.*

I want him to go away, Drest thought, tears filling her eyes. *I don't know what Da did to him, but I've done nothing, and I've only got three more days. Please make him go.*

I can't, lass; I'm in ropes at the castle. Ah, my sweet Drest, if I were with you now, I'd crush that fly. But you must manage on your own.

It was as if the words had truly come from Thorkill in his ropes at Faintree Castle—and they made Drest's heart ache all the more.

Drest dozed, though she tried not to, and woke with a start when she felt the weight of the branch shift on her shoulders. She had no room to draw her sword, packed in as she was against Emerick and Tig. Panic froze her.

Nay, lass, said Gobin's voice, *don't be scared. He expects you to be sleeping. Surprise him with an attack.*

I can't, Gobin.

Don't think. Do what I say: Slip out from under this branch and knock him down. If you're quick enough, you'll have time to draw your sword. Ready, lass?

I don't know if I'm ready. I don't know if I'll ever be ready, Gobin; I'm so tired and—

Don't think. Slip out—now!

Drest pushed up the branch and flung herself against the intruder.

She met a wall of short, warm fur.

Drest fell back.

Enormous startled eyes, glistening and brown, stared down at her.

It was a stag, a kingly one, with a mass of antlers like an overgrown crown. It did not occur to Drest that a stag of that size could end her journey with one blow from those mighty antlers. She was so stunned by its presence that she held out her hand to touch its coat and make sure that it was real.

The fur was soft as down.

With a snort, the stag walked forward and raised its mighty head.

A hooded figure in a long black cloak stepped from the shadows and swung itself up on the stag. The rider's face looked back at Drest from beneath the hood, visible for an instant in the moonlight.

It was Merewen, unsmiling.

The moon went behind the clouds again.

Into the shadows the stag leaped, and soon it was running between the trees with more noise than Drest would have thought a stag could make: breaking branches, rustling leaves—noises, Drest realized with a start, that sounded much like three travelers stumbling through the woods.

She was still motionless by the fallen branch when a shape detached from the branches above her head and jumped down, landing only a few feet away. It was a man's shape, and it reeked of sweat.

"There you go, running off," muttered the man. "You're as much of a coward as your father."

Drest watched him disappear in the path of the stag. She was frozen by his sudden presence but also by the glimpse she'd had of her rescuer.

You're out, you're free, the bandit's running away, and here you're standing like a toad doing nothing, snapped Uwen's voice. *Have you forgotten about us?*

Drest's heart began to pound. She lifted the branch. Tig looked up, blinking, then scrambled out.

"There was a stag here," Drest said. "With Merewen on its back. She saved us, Tig. The bandit's going after *her*, not *us*. Now quick, help me with Emerick."

But the boy didn't move. "Merewen was here? That means she's following us. I wonder what she wants."

"Tig, we haven't time to think of that. We have to get out of these woods!" Drest knelt and drew a limp, groggy Emerick to his feet.

Tig took his place under the young knight's other arm, and soon they were rushing out from the trees and onto the road.

◂ 20 ▸

THE DEAD

They walked down the road all night, no longer worried about the bandit, thanks to Merewen and her stag. Drest felt even better when they came upon the crest of a hill and saw the next town. It was not far down the slope, encircled by a wooden wall.

"Thank God," said Emerick. "Let us beg some food here, food and a wash; I could eat a whole boar, tusks and all, and I'm as filthy as one too."

Emerick had been quiet all that night. Drest was heartened by the return of his old manner.

"I could eat five boars," she said, "but we can't stop."

"If we find a boar, we'll roast and eat it as we walk," Emerick said. "Agreed?"

Drest grinned. "Agreed."

"Tig?"

"I'll carry it for you." The boy slipped away from Emerick and, cheeks blown out, pretended to stagger beneath an awkward and heavy burden.

They walked down the hill and approached a gate made of densely woven sticks that shifted and creaked in the wind.

"This would do little to protect a town, even if it were closed," Emerick said. Then he stopped. "A woven gate, perpetually open, at the foot of a hill. God's bones, I've heard of this place. It's Birrensgate, a town known for its kindness to bandits."

Drest's heart sank. "Should we go around it?"

"Let's go through it as quickly as possible," Emerick said. "There's no reason to make our journey longer. And if we chance upon a bandit, let's pretend to be bandits ourselves and beg for food and water. They eat and wash too, you know."

The three passed through the gate. The rising sun lit the empty path and the dirt-speckled thatched houses that stood close to it. Shutters hung ragged and split. No flowers or grass grew along the road. There was no trace of anything green.

Drest led her companions up to the town square, where a stone well waited, its bucket cracked and dry. "At least there's a well. Let's have a drink. Then I claim the bucket for washing first."

Tig leaned over the opening. He came up, his nose wrinkled. "Not here. Don't even think of drinking or washing from *this* place: There's poison in that well. That's the smell of death, my friends. And not a quick or easy one."

Drest leaned over and sniffed—and winced at once at the stench of rotten meat. "That's enough to make me sick. Is there other water, do you think? A river or a stream?"

From Tig's shoulder, Mordag made a low sound like a growl, then shot into the sky, then beyond the houses.

Her harsh caw rang out over the empty town.

"Is it the bandit?" In her heart, Drest begged for the answer she was sure she would not get.

Tig's face was tense. "He must be on the road behind us. I don't know how he caught up to us. Shall I attempt to—"

"Nay, let's go back there," Drest said, pointing at the abandoned homes crowding the road.

Quickly, she drew Emerick's arm over her shoulder and led them down a passage between the houses toward a humble hut tucked behind the others. Her companions could sit inside and she could wait at the door with Borawyn drawn. Though she had no energy to fight, it seemed the best option. Drest went to the open door.

"Wait," said Tig. "Not here."

Drest looked around for the source of Tig's warning, then saw it: a pattern of white stones just inside the door, twelve lines forming a star. A single black stone sat in its center.

"What does that mean?" Drest asked.

"It's a village curse. Someone's died in this house. It means that if you enter, you invite death to follow you." Tig shuddered. "Let's find another house."

Drest led them to the doorway of the next.

This house was larger. But on its threshold lay the same pattern of stones, the twelve-pointed star with the black center.

They went to another, then another, their search growing frantic. Every house was marked with the same grim pattern.

"I don't like this," Drest whispered. The urge to flee, to run like mad, was very strong in her.

Emerick stared at the path that wove between the houses back to the square. "It must have been the well. I wonder who could have been so cruel. Poisoning a well is for siege warfare, not villages."

Drest's stomach clenched. "Did everyone in this village drink from that well and die?"

"Not everyone; someone must have buried the dead and set these stones. But it is clear that many perished." The wounded man's hand tightened on her shoulder. "Don't think of it. Let's find a way out of this town."

Staggering, Drest led them farther from the well, until

the three were close to the town's wooden wall. It rose more than twice Emerick's height above their heads.

"It's no good." Emerick set his hand against the bound trunks that formed the wall. "This encircles everything. We must get back to the road. Or find a break in the wall. Tig, can Mordag help us with that?"

The boy reached up and stroked the crow, who had just landed on his shoulder. "She can only tell us where an enemy is. I haven't trained her for anything else."

Drest looked around. The wall extended without any sign of a crack. She had no doubt that she could climb it, but Emerick couldn't.

"Let me confront him," said Tig. "I could draw him off into a chase. I really will this time." He made a feeble effort to smile.

"Nay," said Drest. "It's time for me to end this. Lad, will you help Emerick and get back to the road?"

With a flush of relief, the boy went to the young knight.

"Go behind the houses," Drest said. "I'll catch up when I'm done."

Emerick reached out and touched her shoulder. "What if he harms you?"

She forced a grin that hung heavy on her face. "Do you think a fox-livered bandit can win against Grimbol's daughter?"

"Don't fight him. Talk to him. Please."

At Drest's nod, Emerick and Tig began their unsteady way on a path between two houses, Mordag flapping above them. Soon they were gone.

Remember the code, murmured Nutkin's voice. *Never falter before yourself or the enemy. He doesn't expect you to confront him. That's your advantage.*

It's time, Drest, said Gobin. *Let's show him what our wee lass can do.*

With a deep breath, Drest drew her sword and started back the way they had come.

BIRRENSGATE

The bandit was sitting on the lip of the well. His face was narrow with a scrap of a beard, and he wore a stained tunic and hose ripped at the knee. He slipped off the well and brandished a broad wooden staff as Drest stepped into the square.

Not a staff, Drest saw as she drew closer, just a stick he must have found in the woods.

It was a large stick, though. She would need to take care.

"There you are, girl."

That slippery voice made Drest shiver, as if it were night in the woods again. But Borawyn's weight reminded her to be brave.

Careful, Gobin's voice said in her mind. *He's stronger than you. You'll need to be clever.*

She raised her sword.

The bandit gave a short laugh and returned to his seat on the well. He rested the staff against the stone bricks and began to lower the bucket. "You're smaller than your brothers. Can you really hold that sword upright?"

Drest's ears burned. "Aye. I can swing it too." She gave a short, smooth practice sweep in the air. The sun gleamed on Borawyn's blade.

"It moves like mush in your hands." But the bandit wasn't smiling. "You don't need to threaten me, girl."

Drest took a breath. She remembered Emerick's advice. Could she use words instead of Borawyn? "I think I must threaten you. You've been bothering me."

"Bothering you? Do you call it that? I only saw you in the woods and thought we could talk." The bandit peered into the well at the bucket he was drawing up. "You could have ended this long ago if you'd have come out when I first asked." He stole a swift, predatory glance.

Frighten him, said Nutkin. *He sees just a lass. Show him what you really are.*

Get ready, said Gobin, *just as I taught you.*

Drest grabbed Borawyn with both hands to keep the sword steady. "You say you want to talk, but that's not what my brothers taught me to do when I meet bandits."

A snarl flashed in the bandit's face. "What do they tell you to do? Wobble your sword? Put that down. It's too big for you."

Show him one of our moves, said Gobin.

"You don't know how to hold a sword, do you." Drest's voice came out sharp. "I'll give you a lesson. You want it to wobble because then it strikes quick."

She darted in and swung Borawyn in a clean, complete arc—a sunrise, her favorite move—that would have slashed through anyone unlucky enough to have been standing near.

The bandit's fingers slipped on the bucket, which dropped into the well with a splash.

"It doesn't wobble in attacking," Drest said, bringing the sword to a halt in the air.

The bandit paled, then reddened nearly as quickly. "You put that away. We're having a talk. We'll have a drink. There's no reason to bring a sword into it."

Borawyn's weight bore down on Drest's arms, but she didn't lower it. "There's always a reason to bring a sword into a talk. That's what my da says. Do you know my da? His name is Grimbol. Some people call him the Mad Wolf of the North."

"Don't say that name in this town," the bandit snapped. "The spirits will have your throat."

Drest held in her shudder and set her jaw. "I think any spirits would cower at my da's name just like you're cowering. You look like you're going to make water in your hose."

The bandit's lips drew back. "Watch out, girl."

Drest lowered Borawyn slowly, though her arms were shaking. She hoped the bandit wouldn't notice. "Why? I'm not the one afraid of a name."

"You would be if you knew who I am."

"I know who you are," Drest said. "You're a dirty, smelly bandit who has made a puddle in his hose at my da's name. I never knew someone would do that. Uwen said he saw a man do that in battle, but I didn't believe him before." She lifted her sword again and made a sudden slash in the air. "Do you want to fight?"

"Not here. I'll fight you on the road, but not here."

With a sniff, the bandit settled back on the well and started to draw the bucket up again.

"What's your name?" Drest didn't know what made her ask it, but she felt daring.

"Why do you want to know?"

"You said I'd be frightened if I knew. So I'm asking. Have you a name, or shall I give you one?"

"Jupp," said the bandit. "My name is Jupp. Have you heard it? Your father knows it well."

Drest rested Borawyn's tip in the dirt. "I've never heard that name."

Wonder and fury passed through the bandit's eyes. "He's never told you?"

"Nay, he doesn't talk of bandits but to say that if we see one we should kill it like a rat."

All at once, Jupp rose, his face red, his hands clasped tightly on the staff. And before Drest could prepare, he was running for her.

Quick, lass! Swing it up!

It seemed to be Gobin's hands, not her own, that thrust Borawyn into the air. With a mighty crack, the sword caught the bandit's stick. He was close enough for her to see the veins in his eyes.

But then he fell away, the staff clattering uselessly to the side, and Drest was above him.

Now swing it down! thundered Wulfric's voice, echoing through her head.

What are you waiting for? Gobin's voice, desperate. *It'll take nothing to strike this blow!*

Drest didn't move. Something was holding her back, despite her brothers' voices.

The bandit was on his knees, crawling away, then on his feet, then running behind the well.

What have you done? moaned Gobin. *You squandered that chance!*

Drest lowered her sword, trembling.

"Was that mercy?" The bandit hovered on the other side of the well.

"Maybe I'd like to have a *real* fight," Drest said. She tried to make her voice sound like Emerick's: strong and haughty.

Jupp straightened. "I'd slay you right now if I could."

"Why do you hate me?"

"Anyone who's lived in this town hates your family."

"And my family hates all bandits, but why do *you* hate *me*? Is it because you were a bandit in this town?"

"Villagers, not bandits, lived in this town. And I wasn't always a bandit." Jupp's eyes were hard upon her. "Your father should have told you the story."

"Well, he didn't." Drest hesitated. "Is it your story? Will you tell me it?"

"It's not just my story." Jupp raised his chin, gesturing to the houses behind her. "Years ago, he came into my house, your father. Had a bucket. Poured it into the kettle and said it was for soup. Told me he knew I was tired. He was glad to do the lifting from the well. I'd just done a job for him. I thought he was doing me a kindness. I would never have thought he'd poison our well, nor that he'd give *me* the first taste." Jupp inhaled. "That night, I felt it. Everyone in this town who'd drawn from that well felt it. No one slept. By morning, in all the streets, you could hear nothing but crying. That water—it was strongest on anyone weak or sick or small. My sister and her bairn had been in a fever. They hadn't eaten for days before they ate that soup. That soup—it was the last thing they tasted." His voice was heavy. "That's why I hate you, girl. You're his daughter. I'd put you in my sister's place if I could."

The ground beneath Drest seemed to tremble.

"My da doesn't poison wells," Drest said.

The bandit sniffed. "That's what he tells you, is it. He never told you about Birrensgate. When you see him next, ask him why he did it. I'll never know."

They stood separated by the well and the stretch of bare ground, their eyes never leaving each other.

It's not true, Drest thought. *That's not my da.*

"Go away," Jupp said, his voice a slippery whisper. "I didn't ask you to meet me here."

"Stop following me."

Jupp lowered his gaze, blinking. "Soft. Weak and soft. It's a disgrace."

Drest knew that the bandit wasn't speaking about her.

"Go," whispered Jupp. "Don't make me look at you a moment longer."

She turned and continued on the road through the town, careful not to run. She glanced back at Jupp. He was watching her, though he didn't raise his head. He did not move from his spot.

◄←→►

Emerick and Tig had staggered only just beyond the village's other gate when Drest caught up with them.

"The bandit's still there. He's not going to bother us any longer, though. We had a talk." Drest quickly took her place under Emerick's arm.

Tig pulled away and rubbed his shoulder.

The wounded man leaned on her heavily. "We were worried; we'd heard no sound and wondered if he'd crept up behind you."

"I had to use my sword, but just a bit, and only because he came at me." Drest paused. "I could have slain him and ended this. But I didn't."

"You could have been hurt. I've known few battles where all warriors emerged unscathed." He gave her a weary smile. "Words can be a strong weapon, no? Celestria once told me that."

She nodded. The bandit's words had felt like the strongest weapon yet.

⤙ 22 ⤚

THE PAST

They walked for the rest of the day and into the night, without food or water. Birrensgate whirled in Drest's mind all that time. She could picture her father on a crowded battlefield, his sword raised high. Or home on the headland, his face bright behind the bonfire. She could not see him in Birrensgate, leaning over the well to draw up a bucket of poisoned water.

But what if he had?

When it was dark, Drest built a small fire and knelt to help Emerick sit. He eased himself back slowly, drawing in his breath between his teeth, but at last was settled.

From the stains on his tunic, it was clear that his rib wound had again oozed through its wrappings.

"I'll find some moss to bind that for you," Drest said. "I'll take Tig so we can be quick."

Emerick nodded and gave her a grateful look, then closed his eyes.

Tig followed Drest into the sparse woods near the road.

For the first few minutes, they gathered moss without speaking.

"Something you heard from that bandit is plaguing you," Tig murmured.

"Aye, the past. My da's." Drest peeled up a fist-sized chunk of moss. "It's made people like that bandit hate me."

"It's not your fault, Drest."

"Nay, but it doesn't go away, does it? The past."

Tig set down his moss. "Have you ever known in your heart who you are—not what people tell you, but who you *really* are—and tried to be that? If I could have any power in the world, I'd want it to be the ability to tear away the past."

"I don't think anyone can do that."

"No? Just watch."

Tig pretended to rip something from his shoulders and slapped it on the ground. Then he reached over and pretended to tear something from her shoulders too. He added that to his imaginary pile, and raked a handful of soil over it.

"There. I've taken off my miserable past, and your father's past for you, and buried them. We needn't think of them again."

Drest wanted to smile, but a lump was in her throat. "I'll try, but—but I *am* my da's bairn. A warrior."

"Oh, you're a warrior, but you're not like *him*."

Drest frowned. "How do you know that?"

"Because you ran into a field against six lads to save me, you rescued a witch from a mob, you're hauling your enemy around as if he's your greatest friend—"

"The last part's for the trade, lad, and the rest are all things my brothers would have done."

"You do more: Not slaying your bandit, going after your family like this—Drest, you're the kindest person I've met."

"Nay, I'm not. It's just my da's code."

"Does it tell you to be a warrior with a good heart? No, that's your own doing. That's what makes you a legend."

"I don't know what you mean by that." Drest's face was hot.

Drest has an admirer, giggled Uwen's voice.

Shut it, rumbled Gobin.

Nay, she does. A wee admirer with arms like twigs.

Shut it, came Gobin's voice, harder this time. *And you should know better than to ignore my word.*

"We should return to Emerick," Tig said, rising. "I think this is all the moss we'll get."

Even before they emerged from the trees, Drest saw Jupp on the road, standing far too close to Emerick. The wounded man had propped himself up but was clearly helpless.

She dropped the moss, drew Borawyn, and bolted

157

toward the bandit as fast as she could. "You broke your promise!"

Before she reached him, she lunged. The heavy sword only wobbled slightly this time.

Jupp leaped beyond the blade's reach. "I made no promise and I meant no harm. I was only wondering if you might share your fire and meal with another traveler on these roads."

"There's not enough fire to share. And there's nothing else here but my wounded friend, and no one touches him." Drest swung her sword down, narrowly missing Jupp's legs.

The bandit backed away. "I don't know why you hate me, girl. I thought we had an understanding."

"Aye, I thought so too: You said you'd stop following."

The bandit retreated into the shadows beside the road. "I wasn't following; I'm going my own way. Now let me pass."

"Coward. Go back to where you came from."

"I've nowhere to go but ahead. Launceford—it's a full night's walk—that's where I'm going. It's where I live. I only want to get home."

"You said in the woods that you were watching me, that you'd seen me grow up. Launceford's far from the headland; it's not your home."

Drest was about to lunge at him again when Emerick's weak voice stopped her.

"Let him pass. He wants only warmth and food. I've told him we have neither. Let him pass and find his own."

Drest shook her head; she didn't want the bandit ahead of them.

But Jupp took Emerick's words to heart. "I will go straight on and walk all night," he said, "and I thank your wounded friend." With that, he strode away up the road into the darkness.

Drest held her sword aloft. "He's going to wait for us."

"I'm sorry, Drest; I had to speak. He had a dagger you didn't see. He was readying it for the next time you lunged. When you are close to a man, a dagger is a better weapon that a sword."

A wave of cold passed through Drest. She went to Emerick's side. To her surprise, he reached out and took her hand.

Tig came to Drest's other side. His face was utterly white.

She settled down to add the little moss they had collected to Emerick's bandages and tried to think of anything but Jupp's vengeful face. But she was tired. She was also desperately thirsty, and hungry; the hearth bread and ale from the day before were a distant, sweet memory. And it was night. In two days, her father and brothers would be hanged. She had to keep moving and not worry about the bandit waiting farther along on the road.

Then Drest thought of the stones in the doorways of Birrensgate and of the bandit's story.

"His name is Jupp," Drest said slowly. "That bandit."

"He told you?" Emerick asked.

"Aye. He said my da had poisoned the well. Some of those stones in the doorways were for Jupp's family." She had no wish to speak her next words, but they came out nonetheless. "His sister and her bairn."

Emerick was quiet. Drest was grateful that he didn't remind her of Grimbol's brutality at that moment.

"He grieves them, no doubt," Emerick said at last. "That should surprise no one. They were a family, Jupp and his sister and her child."

"Just like my da and my brothers and me," whispered Drest.

To her shame, hot tears welled in her eyes. And in a moment, she was sobbing.

Emerick's hand closed on her shoulder. Tig's closed on the other.

It took Drest several minutes to stop. She drew away from her companions, wiping her stinging eyes with the back of her hand. "It was building up in me from no food and no rest. But don't worry; a good fire and a doze—"

"That's nothing to be ashamed of," Emerick said. "Faintree Castle's bravest knights would have done the same after experiencing what you've encountered."

"All the men in Phearsham Ridge cry," said Tig, "more often than you think."

"I can't afford to cry," Drest said, and took a long breath.

There was so little time, but the travelers settled down for the night. Not one of them could walk any farther.

Tig had agreed to watch for half the night, but when Drest was ready to wake him, her thoughts had not quieted enough to let her sleep. Indeed, they had grown ever fiercer.

Why would Grimbol poison Birrensgate?

What had Jupp done to evoke such fury?

What had truly happened to the lady Celestria?

They were all questions for her father, but she didn't know if she'd be able to speak them aloud when she saw him next.

If she saw him.

Two days more.

What if the bandit stopped them again?

What if Emerick's wounds were too painful for him to move?

What if *she* couldn't move, tired and hungry, her nerves raw with fear?

What if she couldn't do it?

Don't think of that, lass.

It was her father's voice. For the first time.

Drest opened her eyes. The fire was huge and bright. Darkness hung behind it, as dense as the sea.

You're a good lass to come after us, but it's been a hard journey, and the hardest part yet is to come. Steel yourself, Drest, and never forget who you are.

Da, all those things the bandit said—

Let's not talk of that. Let's not think of that. You've one matter before you, and you must set your mind to that alone. Aye, lass, this is battle, and you cannot let yourself be distracted.

Drest slowly nodded. *Can you tell me what I should do when I reach the castle, Da?*

To rescue us? Nay, lass, you must find your own way, just as you've done all this time.

Drest's heart was suddenly pounding. *Won't you or the lads be there for me?*

Nay, lass. Not as you think you need us. Now wake that lad and tell him it's his turn to watch. You need your sleep and strength for the days ahead. But don't rest too long, my girl; you've only two days.

⤙ 23 ⤚

LAUNCEFORD

Drest, Emerick, and Tig rose before dawn on the road beyond Birrensgate with dry throats and hollow stomachs. Drest had been hungry and thirsty before, but never like this, and she suspected the feeling was worse for her companions.

"Lass, do you remember that brook in the woods that you found by the sea?" Emerick's voice was weak. "Might you find another?"

She had to; they could not go on without water.

Drest led her companions into the woods. Maybe she could find an alder: the tree, she knew, that always grew near water. Emerick, supported by a stumbling Tig, trailed behind as she looked for a trickle, a patch of grass, anything damp. There were no alders, only dry pines, and a scattering of oaks. But at last, Drest found a deep crevice in a lightning-damaged oak where rain had collected. It smelled clean and tasted only slightly of wood.

The three scooped the water from the hollow with their

hands and drank, over and over, until the water was gone. Then they tramped back to the road.

That day was the hardest yet. The sky was clear but the forest was thick around them: perfect terrain for a bandit to hide. No one spoke, and Emerick leaned more and more on Drest and Tig. By midday, he was holding his breath with every step, just as he had when Drest had taken off his hauberk in the ravine. It was hard to keep going, but the three trudged on, pausing only when Emerick grew too tired to continue.

As the sun began to set, a town's great iron gates appeared in the distance. From the road ahead came horses, carts and wagons, and people on foot, all entering the town.

"At last," breathed Emerick. "This is Launceford. We are nearly at the castle. But let's stop. We need food."

"And water," added Tig. "You said at Birrensgate that you could eat a boar. Well, I could drink an ocean. In one gulp."

"I want both those things as much as you, but we don't have time," Drest said. "We've only one more day." Her stomach twisted.

"We'll make it, Drest, I promise," said Emerick. "If we eat and rest only briefly, we'll have the strength to walk all night and reach it by dawn."

The three approached the town gate and joined the flow of people and carts from the other direction. They stepped in behind a pair of pilgrims in dusty brown robes.

"That's the dangerous way," one of the pilgrims was saying to his companion, pointing down the road from which Drest and her friends had come. "It's thronged with bandits, and, if you go the whole distance, they say you'll come upon the Mad Wolf's lair."

"I heard there was a cozy little town some distance from here—what was it called? Some pointy name—whose healer could do wonders for a limp." The pilgrim patted his leg.

"Phearsham Ridge," said the other. "Yes, we should go there. And we can ask one of the villagers to show us the path through the woods, for there is a trail that will take us to the other road and far from the Mad Wolf."

"Need we worry about him?"

"I think it would be wise to avoid his lands even now. Remember what they said? There is still a wolf cub loose."

Emerick leaned heavily on Drest and reached his good arm forward, touching one of the pilgrims on the shoulder. Both turned around, their eyes sharp but more curious than suspicious.

"Forgive my interruption, good pilgrims," Emerick said in what Drest had grown to think of as his smoothest castle voice, "but I would think from your words that you have recently been to Faintree Castle. I have heard that the Mad Wolf of the North and his sons have been captured and are to be hanged. Has it happened?"

Drest held her breath.

"Not yet," the first pilgrim said. "The hangings are planned for the day after the morrow. There'll be an Easter feast, then the hanging, a proper celebration."

Drest breathed.

"I am glad to hear we still have time," Emerick said. "We have been hastening to the castle to be present."

"I should think you'll make it," the second pilgrim said kindly.

It was the pilgrims' turn to enter the gate. Emerick walked close to them, his head bowed, with Drest and Tig under his arms. The guard barely noticed them. Tig's crow had left them as they joined the line, swooping over the massive stone wall that enclosed Launceford.

Drest tried to keep her senses sharp, but the crowd, the tall houses, and all the smells of food and refuse overwhelmed her. Her brothers had told her stories of large, bustling towns, but she had never imagined there could be so many moving bodies, so much noise, so much stink. And those stone walls surrounding everything, visible wherever they went—it felt like a trap.

They found the town well and drank, gulping the water, taking turns from the bucket. When they were done, Drest caught a whiff of roasting pork from a cook fire nearby.

"I wonder if we might beg a bite of their meal," Emerick said.

They staggered over to the man and woman who crouched beside the fire, but were rebuffed with an answer that was to repeat itself throughout the town: The couple wanted silver. They meant coins, Drest realized, like the ones that padded the treasure bags in the headland's cave.

The marketplace was the same. Everyone asked for silver. Drest grew so sick of hearing it that she was tempted to draw her sword and force a butcher to hand over a lamb carcass.

Eventually, they gave up and searched for a place to rest. On the ground past the market street, the three found an unoccupied space. Emerick was sweating and pale. There was no spot to lean upon, so he lay on his back with his head in the dust.

"If I weren't so covered with blood and dirt, I'd go to the richest house in town and demand a proper meal," Emerick said. "Yet as I am, I'd be taken for a bandit."

"Not you," Tig said. "Bandits are cleaner."

Emerick turned his head on the ground and gazed at

Drest and Tig. "I wonder which of you would be more fit to sell a ring."

"What ring?" Drest asked.

"I have one in my boot. When we were at your camp, I hid it there while you were searching for a boat. My left boot. Go ahead and see if you can find it."

The boot was heavy and muddy and would not come off.

"It smells worse than sea rot," Drest muttered. "Has a wee animal crawled in there and died?"

She dug her heels into the dirt, gave the boot a mighty heave, and almost fell backward when it slid free. She turned it upside down, and a gold ring fell out.

The ring was dull but carved intricately. Turning it in her fingers, Drest could just make out the pattern of a tree.

"That ring is worth a mighty sum," Tig said, peering over Drest's shoulder as she set it in Emerick's hand.

"It was my father's." Emerick fingered it. "I don't want to give it up, but it will pay for the food we desperately need. And a horse. See, Drest, how eager I am to be traded for one of your brothers?"

"I can fetch us food when it's darker. You don't have to sell your father's ring."

Tig held out his hand toward Emerick. "Let me sell it. I

know how to barter, how to outsmart anyone. I'll find the goldsmith and trade it to him for everything we need."

Emerick dropped the ring in his hand. "Be careful, Tig."

The boy winked at Drest. "Lads on quests don't need to be careful; we always escape true danger, thanks to our friends."

With the ring tight in his hand, he sauntered off.

Drest eased herself beside Emerick and stretched out her legs. She didn't like to see Tig disappear alone like that; worry tugged at her. "I'm sorry I didn't think to fetch coins. We have plenty of them at the headland and I know all the spots where they're hidden."

"They would have sunk to the bottom of the sea when our boat cracked open. But that doesn't matter; my ring will buy us the best horse this town can offer and we'll reach the castle in mere hours."

Drest scuffed the worn toe of one boot in the dirt. Thinking of rescuing her family now, it seemed impossible. What would she do in the castle with just one brother against a band of knights?

"I know you said I could have one brother for you, but what about the rest of my family?" Drest said. "I can't let them die."

"I can't do anything about the rest of them. It will be difficult enough to free one. And there is to be a crowd. A celebration." The young knight frowned. "For good reason, but still."

Drest sat up. "What about the knight who tried to murder you? He'll be there, you know."

Emerick met her eyes. "You don't need to worry about that," he said coldly.

"Nay, but if we free my whole family together, they'll protect you. If you can lead me to where they're being kept—"

"Absolutely not." Emerick's voice changed back to the stern castle voice he had used on the headland. "Your father and brothers are murderers many times over. I shouldn't even be talking about this."

Drest rose, her face burning. "I'm going to look for Tig. Selling a ring shouldn't take this long."

She expected a protest, a warning to be careful, or at least a nod. But Emerick didn't even raise his eyes as she turned away.

Drest kept to the shadows and made her way toward a chorus of shouting voices in the market road. Someone there could surely tell her where the goldsmith's house was, but the crowd's clamor reminded her of the mob that had surrounded Merewen in Soggyweald.

A sharp caw sounded above Drest's head. Tig's crow was clinging to a rooftop, distinct against the early night, her beak pointing to the throng.

"I don't like crowds," Drest muttered. "If you're teasing me, I'll have one of your wings."

As if she could hear Drest, Mordag uttered a disgruntled *creea*.

With a prickling sense of dread, Drest slipped among the people.

Men and women were pushing one another and talking about getting close. Drest felt like a fly among them. She crawled through the spaces until she was near the front of the crowd.

Grimbol had once told her about village stocks, a cruel form of humiliation. Drest had often wondered how two strips of wood could hold any man. But seeing the stocks of Launceford, she understood. They were like a pair of jaws that had closed upon their victim.

And their victim in the center of the market square was Tig.

⤙ 24 ⤚

THE STOCKS

Resentment and fear streaked Tig's face. He hung limp in the stocks, his hands and head secured in the three wooden holes. Before him, a man in a green cloak was bellowing a charge:

"And for this theft he shall spend two nights and two days in punishment. Let him learn the error of his ways."

The crowd grumbled. Drest, who had hated every person within it, was surprised. Were they so tenderhearted?

But it turned out that the people in the crowd cared little for the boy: They were there to see what he had stolen. As if they were of one body, they followed the man in the green cloak as he strode away.

Drest pulled back from the throng and waited until they were well down the road before she ran to Tig's side. "What happened, lad?"

Tig grimaced. "May he swallow that ring and choke on it. The goldsmith—the brute, the monster—he *stole* it from me. As soon as I held it out. I knew he'd try to trick me, but

I never suspected he'd just *take* it! He took it and called the bailiff. I couldn't escape." Tig rattled the stocks. "I am *not* a thief! I never was!"

Drest pulled at the wood. It didn't budge. "We have to get you out. We can't wait two days."

"Especially since they said they'll hang me after that." He gave her a grim smile. "It's time for you to protect me."

Drest walked around the stocks, tracing every crack and line with her fingers. The pieces fit together as tight as stone, secured by wooden pegs shoved into metal clasps. Drest found a rock in the dust and pounded at the pegs and clasps. But she could move nothing.

She sat back on her heels. There had to be a crack where she could slip in her sword, some place where the wood joined and would give. She saw only three such places: the holes that encircled Tig's neck and wrists. It was dangerous, but Borawyn just might force that wood apart.

"I shall break this open with my sword," Drest said.

"Is that wise?"

"I don't know, but I'm sure I can do it. Hold still."

The boy's eyes had been following her as much as they could around the stocks, but at that moment, they widened.

"Duck!" Tig cried.

Drest ducked, and just in time.

"Get away from the prisoner." A man in a cabbage-shaped wool cap launched a blow at Drest's face.

She dodged, sprang past him, and scampered into an alley by the buildings around the square. The cabbage-headed man marched toward her, swinging a long staff.

Drest tried to think. She needed Emerick to distract the guard. Why was the young knight so useless? Worse than useless.

He'll be useful enough when you reach the castle, said Gobin's voice.

Tig's guard was heading toward her, his staff thumping.

Drest circled around and went back to the road. Once there, she ran across, and waited in the shadows until Tig's guard moved farther up the square.

She glanced up to see if Mordag was still watching Tig. To Drest's surprise, the crow was on a different roof, looking in a different direction.

Where Emerick was waiting.

Drest ran past the market road to the spot where she had left the wounded man.

The ground was empty.

She walked farther, but the houses became unfamiliar. She returned to the market road, then traced her way back until she was once more standing on the spot where Emerick had been lying on the ground.

A flicker of movement appeared near the corner of a house, then was gone.

Emerick, Drest thought, and ran around the corner.

Emerick wasn't alone. He was on his feet, his head forced back against Jupp's shoulder. One of the bandit's hands held him in place. The other held a dagger to his throat.

✦ 25 ✦

JUPP'S REVENGE

"Run," Emerick's lips and eyes both said, though he did not speak the word aloud.

"I was wondering how long you'd take," said Jupp. His voice was hard and low, no longer slippery. "Didn't find a way to free the boy, did you? I was counting on seeing you draw that sword and chop those stocks in two."

Drest stood very still. Her hands longed to whip Borawyn free, but the bandit's knife was firm against Emerick's throat.

"Your friend here claims he's got nothing of value about his person," Jupp went on, "and he certainly has nothing I can find. But you're another matter."

"I've nothing on me, either, unless you want a smelly boot," Drest said, trying to sound brave.

"You *lie*." Jupp's tongue ran over his bottom lip. "Give me that sword, and I'll free your friend."

Drest almost drew in her breath, but she knew better than to show surprise. "I don't know why you care about this old thing," she managed to get out. "It's a piece of scrap."

"You showed it to me well enough before. Give it here." Jupp set the knife against the center of Emerick's throat and angled it to one side, as if he were about to slash.

"Maybe it's worth something," Drest said quickly, "but it's my brother Wulfric's sword. He's on my path to get it back and if he finds someone else has taken it, he'll—"

"Do you think I don't know where your brothers are? Don't lie to me again, girl. I can see right through it."

"Don't give it to him," Emerick said, his eyes burning into Drest. "Go away with Tig. Do it now."

The bandit laughed. "You don't know? Your boy is in the stocks, put there for stealing a ring, they say."

There was a subtle change in Emerick's face: a flash of despair, then nothing.

"I don't see that you have much of a choice." Jupp dug his fingers into Emerick's shoulder, which made the young knight gasp. "Wounded here too, are you?"

She had no time to think of her brothers. Drest drew her sword and threw it to the ground. It landed in the dust with a muted clatter.

"Pick it up," Jupp said, "and hand it to me."

Without looking at Emerick, Drest obeyed. She held Borawyn out by the crossguard, the blade pointed down.

Jupp reached forward, his knife still against Emerick's throat, and snatched the sword from Drest's grip.

Then he flung it aside. He threw Emerick down and landed a kick in his ribs that made the young knight double up in pain. Before Drest could move, Jupp's hands were upon her, twisting her arms back.

"I made a mistake, pitying you, as if you needed pity." The bandit shoved his knee into her spine and forced her to the ground. "You're the whelp of a devil. When I saw you alone in the woods—there was my chance. To grab you. To show your father what it feels like to lose someone."

A net of frantic terror seized Drest. She struggled, and might have thrown him off, but the bandit grabbed his dagger from where he'd dropped it and whipped it beneath her chin.

"Are you going to beg for mercy, you filthy worm? I haven't decided if I'll slay you now or sell you to the highest bidder—yes, there are many who would buy Grimbol's daughter. Yet *I* should slay you. For my sister."

Drest couldn't move.

Nay, lass, whispered Gobin's voice, faint in her mind. *You can't give up.*

Remember the code: Never accept defeat, murmured Nutkin.

Do it, Drest, choked Uwen's voice. *Do it.*

Drest took a quick breath, then reared up.

The bandit's grip on her wrists slipped, but then he had her again and all his weight was on her back. His knife pressed under her chin. The blade was warm.

"You don't want to jostle me, girl. Steady now. I've one thing I need to do before I make my choice. Do you know what it is? I want your ear. I'll put it on a rope and wear it round my neck." He gave a strangled laugh. "A tale for the fireside: how I caught the Wolf's daughter."

Blind panic rippled through Drest. Pressing her fingers into the packed dirt, she forced herself to be still.

"Which shall it be? Left ear or right?"

The knife stung her neck.

"Steady," hissed the bandit. With his fingers suddenly deep in her hair, he thrust her face against the dirt and moved the knife up her right cheek toward her ear.

"Wait." It was Emerick's voice, his castle voice, low and strong. He was moving, dragging himself closer. "Was your sister a brave lass? Were you proud of her? Did she hold you when you were scared? Did you laugh with her when she teased you?" The young knight's voice was like a whip. "The Mad Wolf murdered a girl I loved who did all those things with me. Yet I see what his daughter is: just a lass, nothing more. She could be your sister. She should be no part of your revenge."

Jupp let out a snarl. "She's Grimbol's daughter, not a lass but a demon like him."

But his knife lifted, just barely.

"Did *her* hand poison your village's well? I know it was not *her* sword that slew the lass I loved."

"Shut it." But Jupp's voice was weaker.

"If you slay the Mad Wolf's daughter, you're living by his code, not your own," Emerick said.

"You're a fool not to have slain her when you had the chance," the bandit growled.

Drest raised her eyes. She could barely see Emerick's face. He was pale, but his gaze was firm.

"I had few chances," Emerick said. "I thought of it once, but I've been powerless with my wounds. She's had every reason to slay *me*: I was with the knights who took her family."

"Then I have your men to thank," muttered Jupp. But his knife moved farther from Drest's cheek. "What were you thinking, you filthy grub? Why did you not slay this man? Haven't you the vicious blood of your father coursing through your veins? Answer me."

Drest swallowed hard. "Nay," she said, her voice thick, "I'm not a bloodthirsty villain. I only pretend to be." Her voice broke on the final word.

Silence. The bandit's knee was driving a hollow point of

pain into her back. Drest's cheek was hot and damp against the ground. From the corner of her eye, she could see Jupp's knife trembling.

"Blast," muttered the bandit.

And then the pressure of his knee was gone, along with his weight from her back.

Drest turned over as the bandit rose. He slunk into the shadows, his face contorted in despair.

"This is my one act of mercy, you worm. I owe you nothing." He gave a hollow gasp. "Look at me, loyal at the end. Tell your father what I've done. Tell him that I never— that I—that I've always been loyal."

With a strangled sob, the bandit crept away, and then was gone.

Emerick began to rise, but stopped, caught by a spasm of pain. "Drest," he asked through clenched teeth, "are you hurt?"

She sprang to her feet and caught Emerick as he toppled. "You'll open up all your wounds if you try to get up like that. What's wrong with you? Haven't you learned?"

Wordlessly, he leaned against her, breathing hard. Drest was panting too, her mind in a fog. She had never been so close to harm, so helpless.

"You are a brave, brave lass," Emerick said. "Did he hurt you?"

"I never—I thought—I was sure that only a sword would stop him," Drest said. "He's lucky you didn't grab Borawyn and swing it at his head in that way you knights like to swing."

The young knight winced. "I'm lucky I didn't try. Did he cut you?"

"Nay, just a wee bit on my neck, but it's no matter." Drest paused. "How did you do that? I was sure I was going to die just then."

Emerick smiled faintly. "He wanted to hurt your father, but he wasn't a beast; or at least I was praying he wasn't. To be honest, I wasn't sure if it would work. Thank God it did. Will you help me get up?"

Drest guided his arm around her shoulder and drew him to his feet.

"Is it true that Tig is in the stocks?" the young knight asked once he could breathe again.

"Aye, they stole your ring and put him there."

"Then let's break him out. We'll find out soon enough what monsters are lurking *there*, so take up your sword."

With shaking hands, Drest picked up Borawyn and slipped it into its scabbard.

And with that, the two hobbled toward the market square.

← 26 →

ESCAPE

"You seem to care a lot about your captive," Emerick said as they crept into the street. "You were willing to give up your beloved sword for me."

"You seem to care a lot about your captor. You could have let him kill me." Drest shivered.

"That's not the fate that should meet *my* captor. Someone else's, perhaps."

They could see the stocks now. The marketplace stalls were abandoned and Tig stood silently in his imprisonment. Drest started toward him, but Emerick's grip held her back.

"We must decide what to do. Stocks don't break easily." Emerick sighed. "At least the marketplace is empty. It's cruel to leave him here at night, but better that than start this in the day when people are likely to throw stones."

Drest set her hand on her sword, but her trembling fingers slipped off the wide pommel. "I'm too tired to hack it away. If I give you my sword—"

"Drest, I can't move without your help just now."

"What if I took you over there and—" She broke off.

Two small figures had appeared across the street. They were creeping up toward the market square with frequent starts and stops.

"Do you see them?" Emerick nodded in the children's direction. "Apparently it's not safe at night, either."

Drest tensed. The small figures were closer now to Tig. "You'll have to lean against this wall. Tig needs my help."

"Are you mad, Drest? They surely have knives, and— look at you, you're shaking."

"I promised Tig I'd protect him."

Drest staggered out from the shadows, the sword on her hip much heavier than it had ever been.

The figures turned toward her movement.

Girls. Young, as she had been not long ago.

Drest walked toward them as if she were approaching a pair of fox kits. Their long tunics were tattered, their faces speckled with dirt, and their hair snarled and tangled.

They were watching her with wide eyes.

As if she were a legend come to life.

The Mad Wolf's daughter crouched in the dirt before them. "You there. I wonder if you know about stocks and how to break them to pieces, for that's what I intend to do."

The two children whispered to each other.

"I bet you'd like to see that," Drest said. "People you've loved have been trapped in those stocks, have they not? Perhaps you'd like to see those stocks ripped apart and wrecked forever." Drest nodded toward the center of the square. "That lad is my friend. Will you help me free him?"

They whispered again. One of the girls crept closer.

"What shall we do?"

In those four words, eagerness blossomed—and not just eagerness, but hope. The words revealed a lifetime of humiliation, of need and want and unfair punishment. Drest heard that as clearly as if the children had told her of the life they led in the alleys of Launceford. Seeing the stocks destroyed before their own eyes would prove that life could change.

Drest pointed at Emerick, a bent figure in the distance. "My other friend across the road is keeping watch for us. Come with me and let's think how to free my lad. I'd like to chop that wood in two, but I don't want to hurt him."

"You'd better do it quickly," said the girl who had stayed back. "They're fetching a river boy as guard."

Drest didn't ask what a river boy was; she had an uneasy feeling that one would not be a welcome companion for Tig.

Without looking to see if the girls were following, Drest strode up to the stocks.

Tig cocked his head as best as he could. "You're back. With reinforcements."

"Aye, I promised, did I not?" Drest drew Borawyn. "We're going to free you now, aren't we, lasses?"

She turned then, and found the girls behind her. Their faces shone in the faint moonlight, gazing with wonder upon her sword.

"Are you a girl?" one of them said.

"Aye, just like you."

"You're allowed to have a sword?"

"Aye; my brothers trained me to use it. But I know how to use it in battle, see, not against a wooden brute like this. Do you have an idea of how I can chop it?"

The girls dashed up to the stocks and ran their hands over the wood.

"Chop here," one of the girls said, pointing a dirty finger at Tig's wrist. "The wood is thin."

"But she'll cut off her friend's hand," said the other, "you pignut."

"Nay, you rotten egg, the wood is thin, so she could chop it quick."

"You're both right," Drest said. "What do you think, Tig?"

The boy rattled his wrists against the holes that held them. "None of this feels weak. It was designed to hold men like your brothers. But the hinges—and your sword—can't steel cut through other metals?"

Instantly, the two girls went to the metal clasps and ran their fingers over them. "This one first," said each of them, stroking her chosen clasp. "This one."

Drest took a deep breath. She would have to hold the sword steady, and her aim would have to be perfect.

"Look at your other friend," whispered one of the girls.

Drest turned.

Emerick was gesturing for her to come back.

"Someone's coming," said the other. Both looked to Drest, their eyes doubtful.

"Then do it," said Tig. "Do it *now*."

Drest stood back. Clutching the grip with both hands, she swung Borawyn up, around, and down with all her strength.

The tiny metal hinge snapped off and clinked to the ground.

Drest looked at Emerick again. His gestures were more frantic.

"Quickly, Drest!" said Tig. "The other!"

With a grunt, she swung her sword.

The second hinge broke free at the touch of the blade.

The girls rushed up to the stocks and lifted the loose piece of wood that held Tig's neck and wrists.

Drest sheathed her sword as Tig scrambled out. She turned to the girls. "Take as much wood as you can carry so they can't easily build this again, and run. Tell your family this was a gift—from Drest, the Mad Wolf's daughter."

They scattered: the girls to the shadows, each with her arms filled with pieces of wood; and Drest and Tig to where Emerick was nervously waiting.

"We must flee," said Emerick. "Someone's coming."

The man in green was on the road with a tall boy at his side.

Drest drew Emerick's arm over her shoulders and she and Tig pulled him into the alley. They ducked between houses, into another alley, and kept going like that until grass replaced the houses and the town's stone wall stood before them. Tracing her way through the weeds, Drest followed that wall until the houses became sparse and she saw the iron gates ahead.

They were shut. A guard stood in their shadows, watching the road beyond.

Any moment, someone would find the broken stocks. A call would sound. A hunt would begin. Any moment, they'd be caught.

Then Drest heard it: a faint trickle of water.

She led them through the high grass, parallel to the wall, the sound growing louder, until she saw a rush of familiar dark movement at the bottom of the stone wall.

"A hole," Drest said. "There's a drain hole under that wall, and the water is rushing through. Emerick, can you swim?"

"Not with these wounds."

"But it's our only way out. We have to try."

A man's voice bellowed from the marketplace. Another answered.

Drest and Tig tore through the grass, dragging Emerick. More voices shouted beyond the houses, matching the noise of the water as Drest drew up to the wall.

"Wait here," Drest whispered to Emerick. "Come, Tig. You go first."

She slipped into the icy water, pulling the boy after her. It was slimy and filthy. She couldn't see the hole, but she could feel the rush of water through it, and ducked under to find the edges.

The hole was ragged, rough with broken stones, but large, easily large enough for a boy and perhaps even large enough for a man.

"Tig, can you swim?"

The boy winced, and shook his head.

Drest seized his hand. "Hold on for your life, then."

She ducked deep, pulling Tig through.

The other side shot the water out into a stagnant moat.

Drest swam hard with one arm, drawing a coughing Tig through the water beside her with the other. She swam six strong strokes and pushed the lad to the opposite bank, where he scrambled up. The moon shone over the empty road behind him and the gates in the other direction.

"Keep low and quiet," Drest said, then slid back into the moat.

It took greater effort to swim against the pouring water. Drest had to grasp the edges of the hole to pull herself through. Emerick was already in the water, wading up to his chest, his hand against the stones above his head.

"They're coming, Drest. They're coming along the wall."

"Then hold your breath. Ready?"

Emerick nodded, and inhaled.

Drest pulled him down, under the water, into the hole, and guided his head and shoulders through. The wounded man sank in the moat on the other side. Drest dove after him. She clutched his good arm and swam.

Six strokes again, and they were at the bank. Tig helped her haul Emerick up and to his feet. And together they stumbled, away from the gatehouse, away from the town.

⤛ 27 ⤜

THE WITCH'S GIFT

"Can we stop?"

The wind tore away Emerick's words, but Drest heard them—barely.

"Aye," she said. "We're far enough now."

The three halted, breathing hard, still soaked from the moat. The road hung black and empty around them. Gusts of icy air whipped across the moonlit meadows on either side, chilling them to their bones.

"Might we have a fire?" Tig said, his jaw shaking. "It would make everything so cozy."

Drest eased Emerick to the ground while Tig gathered twigs for tinder. She sank to her knees before the small pile and with trembling hands took her steel piece from her pouch.

"Here." Tig handed her a stone. "This one's nice."

Emerick lay on his back, his fists clenched against his shivers, while Drest raked her chunk of steel against the stone. A few sparks fell, but the wind gusted and blew them out. She leaned over the twigs and tried once more.

A single spark fell, and widened into flame. In seconds, the tinder began to burn.

"Well done." Tig yawned, and curled up beside Emerick.

Drest added more sticks. When the fire was high, she lay down with her friends, her legs and shoulders aching.

She needed to sleep. Yet she had only one more day— two if that pilgrim was right. Her father and brothers were waiting.

Scraps of images filled her head: Jupp's tormented eyes; those frightened, eager children; Tig's furious face in the stocks. And Emerick, his eyes fixed on Jupp, his voice low and steady, somehow at that moment nobler than she could have ever imagined.

Drest looked up. The road stretched empty behind her like the sea. The sea, the headland, and her father too—all seemed so far away.

She closed her eyes, but woke in what seemed to be only seconds later. The fire had snuffed itself out, leaving behind a wispy trail of smoke; and the silver-white moon had risen above the black-tipped trees at the edge of the meadows.

Then she heard it: hooves on the road from Launceford.

Drest started. Someone was coming after them on a horse.

She looked at her companions. Tig was limp with sleep, and Emerick was shuddering with every breath. They were in no state to flee, and the meadows gave them no place to hide. She could only hope that the rider would not notice them in the intermittent moonlight, or would see them only as a bundle of ragged travelers.

The hoofbeats were getting close.

Drest scrambled to her feet and slid Borawyn from its scabbard.

A cloud shifted away from the moon, lighting the road, and she saw the rider who was drawing near: a black-cloaked figure on the massive, antlered stag.

Merewen. Drest lowered her sword with a rush of relief.

The stag slowed, drew even with her, then stopped.

Gray eyes gazed down at her from under the shadowing hood.

"I saw your bandit on the road, in the other direction," said the witch softly, "and knew you would be here, or slain in Launceford. There was no trace of you in town, but there was a story: of a thief, an escape, and a grubby youth with a sword."

"Aye," said Drest, "that was Tig and me. He didn't steal anything."

"Of course he didn't; that's not his way. But I think I know *your* way. You frightened that bandit for good, didn't you. Your father would be proud."

She gazed in silence upon Drest, then turned around and untied a bound black cloak from her stag.

"Here, this is for you. Have you any idea, Drest, of what lies ahead?"

Drest sheathed her sword and took the bundle. "I've already told you I'm not afraid of anything."

"Perhaps you should be. Do you know what a castle is? A mouth of doom for people like us. A sword flashing. Your life cut down before you feel the blade. If you continue on this journey, you will see that for yourself."

Drest stiffened. "Da wouldn't fall. And I won't, either."

"Your father, child, is mortal. He is as vulnerable to a sword as anyone. And so are you. Think carefully. Do you wish to go on? You will die if you do."

"I don't plan on dying." Drest set her jaw, and tried to hold in her shiver. "I've come this far, and I'm not about to turn back. I thank you for the cloak, but I don't want your advice."

The witch gazed at her, her eyes gleaming in the light of the moon. "I wonder—you are so strong. Could that castle be something else for you?" A faint smile came to her face.

"I thought I'd help you, but you don't need my help, do you. You never did."

The witch leaned over and reached out her hand. It curved around Drest's chin and held her, a gesture both warm and soft.

"I have a boon to ask: Remember me kindly, Drest, as but a witch who tried to help you on your way."

Merewen drew back.

"Good-bye. And good luck."

The stag turned toward Launceford and broke into a trot. Soon it was a run, and they seemed to be flying: back up the road, then into the meadow, and then they were gone.

A pang filled Drest as she watched the witch disappear. Then she shook herself and carried the bundle back to Emerick and Tig. As she slipped it from its rope and began to unfold it, the pang disappeared.

Four round, flat loaves of hearth bread appeared after the first fold, strips of smoked meat between them. After another, a stone jug. After the third, a roasted hen, blackened by a fire. After that, fold after fold of the cloak itself— a huge woolen cloak that would cover all three of them.

The witch must have stolen it all in Launceford.

Drest woke her friends. She did not tell them of

Merewen's strange words, only that she'd come with food for them, and they ate, tearing at the bread and meat like starving animals. They took turns drinking new ale, sweet and cold, from the jug. Soon nothing was left but stains on the cloak.

"Let us doze for another hour," Emerick said. "I pray that this gift will give us the strength to walk for the rest of the night. We are very nearly there."

He was pale, however, despite his smile.

"It will take us just a night?"

"We'll find a crossroads ahead, and by that point it is only an hour by horse to the castle. Even with my slow steps, if we leave soon, we'll be there just past dawn."

"Nay, but it's good that we're careful," said Drest. "We shouldn't rush." But what she meant was that, for the first time, *she* could not rush. Merewen's words had shaken her. For the first time, she was afraid.

That night, it began to rain.

⤙ 28 ⤚

THE CROSSROADS

Drest woke to a thunderclap and a rush of water, as if a bucket had been emptied over her head. She and Tig scrambled to their feet.

"It's only rain," Tig said lightly, water streaming down his face. "Seems like a good time to keep going."

Drest pulled up the cloak, dislodging a pool, then ran to Emerick's side and helped him rise. He was heavy and almost entirely limp, though his hand did close on her shoulder in an approximation of his usual way.

Drest arranged the cloak over her two companions, then ducked under too. The rain pelted down, but the wool proved solid.

"Drest?" Emerick's head lolled against her shoulder. "I don't know how long I'll last."

She hung on to him tightly. "How is that? You said you needed only a wee sleep. You've had sleep. And you've eaten."

"With any luck, I will make it far enough for the trade."

Drest winced. "Nay, Emerick. I'm just taking you home. I'm not trading you. I'll find another way to save my family."

But how she did not know.

They walked through the rest of the night, Drest leading the way, only pausing to prop Emerick up when he started to slip. She skirted around puddles marked with ripples and swells like the sea. Mud spattered over the travelers, their boots became heavy with water, and the rain never stopped.

And then, as the foggy length of morning lightened the sky, they came to a tall gray stone, chiseled with writing. A firmly packed road extended on either side.

"A milestone," said Tig. "We must be at the crossroads."

Emerick could barely nod.

All that way, Drest hadn't worried about keeping Emerick alive. He had lasted as she would have expected a knight to last. But now she wondered how dire his wounds truly were: from the red-faced knights' blows, from Jupp's kick, from the journey itself. Far from the obvious cuts and stabs, other wounds could be festering inside of him.

For the first time, Emerick's death on the road seemed a possibility.

Memories of their journey flashed through her mind: his frowning face, his petty insults, the moment they had started to truly work together, his tight embrace after he had saved her from Jupp. She was sure that something bound them now. As Drest walked forward in the pounding rain, she felt that clearly.

A man with a mule tramped past. Four pilgrims huddled by soon after. Then a workhorse drawing a covered wagon plodded up behind them.

"Tig, hold Emerick." Drest wiggled out from under the cloak. In an instant she was in front of the horse, waving madly.

The driver, an old man with a blanket over his head, pulled his horse to a stop. His gaze flicked from Emerick and Tig to Drest in the pouring rain.

"I beg your pardon," Drest bellowed, her voice cracked and loud, "but my wounded friend is of Lord Faintree's castle and needs to get there soon. If he walks on this road any longer, he'll die."

The old man leaned toward her. "I'm going to the castle and I've room in my wagon for all three of you, as long as you don't mind the hay I'm bringing them."

"Hay?" Drest could think of nothing better than burrowing in soft, dry hay.

Bales and bales were packed beneath blankets, protected by the wagon's solid roof. The farmer helped Drest carve out a spot and then drew Emerick up into the prickly, dry nest. It was tight. Tig scrambled up beside him, but there wasn't room for Drest. The farmer tucked blankets over Tig and Emerick, folding the corners against the hay, then shrouded Drest in another blanket.

"I'm sure you'd like the hay too," the farmer said, "but you'll have to sit with me up front."

"Nay, that you're giving us a ride means the world to me, and—wait." She had just felt Borawyn against her hip. It occurred to her that she might attract notice with the sword at her side. "This is my friend's sword. I was carrying it for him. Let me give it back."

Drest unbuckled her sword-belt and slid Borawyn with its scabbard into the hay.

"Don't do that," murmured Tig.

"Nay, it's safer here," she whispered. "I'll just be in the front. Keep an eye on Emerick and call me if he needs help."

Tig's face was grave. "Drest, a warrior should never be without her weapon."

"Aye, but now I won't draw notice."

Yet as Drest pulled the blanket back over her head and took her place on the front bench, Tig's warning resounded in her heart.

⊰ 29 ⊱

FAINTREE CASTLE

A gust of wind sharp with the scent of salt water whipped against the wet blanket that shielded Drest. The smell was as familiar as home. She bared her face to the biting cold.

The farmer and his passengers were not alone upon the road. More carts, mules, and horsemen had joined them, forming a procession in the dwindling rain. The farmer told her the reason why: They had all come to feast and then watch the Mad Wolf and his sons hang.

Drest cringed at the bloodlust of the villagers around her. Had every one of them suffered from the war-band's ways? Or were they faithful to Lord Faintree beyond all reason? She thought of Arnulf and the villagers of Phearsham Ridge and how loathsome the spectacle would seem to them. She also thought of what Tig had said about the goodness and kindness in her. Was there truly so little of it in others?

She was kind, Tig had said. But kindness would not help her battle knights by herself, nor slip into the prison and break all the chains. She could only follow Emerick inside and hope that no one would notice as she crept off to find her family.

Drest wished she had come up with a better plan.

And she wished that even more when the farmer pointed to the four stone peaks of Faintree Castle's keep rising in the distance.

The packed dirt road transformed into a magnificent earthen bridge over the sea. As the procession rattled along, Drest looked down at the crashing waves below.

Ahead of her, the castle walls rose on the edge of an island, propped upon a crown of steep cliffs. It was a brilliant defense.

The first gatehouse was a solid block of a tower on the outer curtain wall. As they neared it in the line of other carts, Drest noted with a shudder the throng of crossbowmen along the crenellated battlements. Each man wore a helm, a chain mail hauberk, and a white surcoat with a brilliant blue tree—just like the surcoats that Emerick and the red-faced knight had worn.

They drew nearer, and nearer, Drest's stomach tightening all the while. At last the farmer faced the pair of waiting guards.

"I have one of your men in my wagon," the farmer told them. "I picked him up at the crossroads with his lad here and his lad in the back."

"He's badly wounded," Drest told the guards, climbing

down from her seat. *Be brave,* she told herself. "I've done all I can to save him, and he's alive, but he'll need more help than I can give."

"How was he wounded?" a guard asked, walking with her to the back.

"He fell—on rocks in the sea." Drest tried not to wince. She wished Tig were at her side explaining.

The guard looked in the wagon while Drest waited and moved from foot to foot. What if Emerick had died and Tig had not told her?

But the guard emerged and told the farmer to go on, and go on quickly. A fellow guard sprang up to Drest's spot on the wagon's bench, and the wagon rattled past.

"I'm supposed to go with him." Drest watched the wagon disappear beyond the castle's first wall of defense. Tig's alarmed face appeared in the back. "He's going to ask where I am."

"He's not going to ask anything in the state he's in." The guard took Drest's arm none too gently and pulled her through the gate and up to the wall to give the next cart room to approach. "What's your name?"

Drest looked down the road, which ran between two stone walls toward the next gatehouse, another tower between another curtain wall. Battlements topped the passageway. There had to be over fifty knights at the tops of

203

those walls; she'd never imagined there would ever be so many in one place.

"Did you hear me?"

She turned back to the guard. "My name is Drest. My— my father is the miller of Phearsham Ridge. Emerick took me along when he stopped by. I'm to go with him if I am to do what my father promised."

"And what is that?"

"Take care of him."

"He's being taken care of now." The guard glanced at the next cart passing by. "Do you want to see the executions?"

"Aye, but Emerick—"

"Then go along with you. See if you can find someone who will share his tent and you may watch from the grass."

"I promised Emerick—"

"No one calls him that here, and you shouldn't, either. Are you going to find a tent to share or not?"

Drest opened her mouth to argue one last time—and remembered the talisman in her pouch. "If you don't believe that he wants me, then look at this." She fumbled past her steel and stone until she found the wooden token. Drest held it out, her heart pounding.

The guard's eyes widened. He looked again at Drest, and all at once, his eyes changed.

"I know who you are," the guard said. "They say he'd

been chasing the youngest of Grimbol's sons. You are he."

Drest stood very still. "I'm not one of Grimbol's sons. My father's the miller from Phearsham Ridge, like I said."

But it was too late. Before she knew what was happening, Drest had been struck in the stomach with a blow that knocked her to the ground. She began to rise, but a second blow kept her down. Before she could twist away, the guard took her hands and wrenched them back. A burning rope dug into her flesh as he bound her wrists.

"You little beast." The guard pulled her roughly to her feet. "You may go to the devil with the rest of your vicious family. This talisman tells us the truth: It tells us not to trust the one who carries it."

"Wait," Drest snapped. "Emerick told me to give that to you. You need to talk to him. He's not going to be happy about this."

Drest ducked in time to miss the guard's blow. But he got her with his next, on her cheek.

"Didn't you me hear the first time? Don't call him that. He's not that name to you."

Then the guard jerked the Mad Wolf's daughter to her feet and dragged her down the shadowed passageway toward the inner gatehouse.

⊷ 30 ⊶

THE PRISON

Darkness surrounded Drest as the guard thrust her head and then her bound hands down through a trapdoor. His fingers were quick: He tied her ropes to the iron ring bolted to the wall beneath the opening, then grabbed the scruff of her tunic and shoved her through.

She was falling, her legs up and over, before they slammed against the wall, echoing with pain. Her wrists burned and her arms ached at the sudden weight on them.

"Here's your final cub," the guard shouted, his ugly voice resounding over the damp stones. He banged the wooden trapdoor shut above her head. A bar slid into place outside, metal into metal.

Drest had not made a sound when the guard had beaten her, and she made no sound now. Her shock had swept away any instinct to struggle and fight.

"Is that you, Drest, my lass?" Grimbol called, his voice strong from the other end of the prison. "Blast. We'd thought you'd escaped."

Drest looked up, blinking. She could barely see in the

gloom but could just make out her brothers hanging on rings beside her.

A deep murmur came from voices along the wall.

"We were sure you were still out there," Thorkill said mournfully.

"We thought you'd hide on the cliffs or in the ravine," murmured Wulfric, "and slip up any man fool enough to chase you."

"Ah, my lass, my lass," said Grimbol. "This is a true defeat."

A sob rose in Drest's throat. "I tried, Da," she said, her voice breaking. "I tried to trick them. I got all this way."

"You came all this way?" said Gobin, who was hanging closest to her. "Not captured at the headland, then? How did you get all this way, lass?"

"I walked. How else would I have come?"

"I've never heard you sound like *that* before," said Nut-kin from beside his twin.

Gobin leaned as close as his ring would allow. "There's a bruise on your cheek. Did they strike you? What do they think they're doing, hammering away at a wee lass?"

A chorus of voices called out from down the wall:

"Are you hurt, Drest?"

"We'll take care of you. No one's going to lay a finger on you again."

"Ah lass, I'll break the hands that beat you."

"And they call *us* brutes."

Drest looked down the prison at her brothers and last her father, their backs against the slimy stone wall. Their voices were clear, sharp, and, for the first time in days, *real*. They buffeted her like sea winds, tearing away her numbing despair until she was fully with her family, and only with them, in the sea-scented prison.

Something splashed beneath her in the darkness. It took Drest a few seconds to recognize that it was the sea and not a floor and to realize how this prison had been built: a series of rings suspended on the wall above the open water. Even if a prisoner got free, there was only deep water below without any place to hold.

"Of course they beat on our Drest; there are knaves ruling this castle." Grimbol's face gleamed in the gloom. "Knaves who hunger for the suffering of others, blind to courage and loyalty."

Like Emerick, Drest thought.

"Listen to me, my sons and daughter," called Grimbol from down the prison wall. "We have one more chance to prove ourselves. They're hanging us at dawn tomorrow. They'll bind our hands and will bind our throats but this I tell you: If you use all your strength, we may win this battle yet. Strike them. Kick them hard. You'll get blows, you'll get stabbed, but don't go down without your fiercest fight. We'll knock them into the sea, we will, or trample them under our boots. If we must die, we'll take two men with each of us. Faintree Castle will never forget this day. And if any of my children should escape, remember your family and your duty to spill the blood lost from us—to spill it tenfold."

Grimbol's voice droned on like a story, just as it had over the fire on the headland when Drest had leaned against her father and felt his arm around her.

She bit her lip to keep from crying.

"For you, my lads, are no ordinary men: You are Wulfric the Strong, Thorkill the Ready, Gobin the Sly, Nutkin the Swift, Uwen the Wild, and Drest—Drest, you are the youngest and you've had no chance to fight. What name will you have?"

All her brothers' heads turned and looked at her.

Drest swallowed. "Sorry, Da?"

"You're one of us, my girl. What name shall I give you? Drest the Quick? Drest the Brave?"

"I'm not brave, Da. Nor quick enough."

The prison was quiet with only the faint slosh of the waves beneath their feet.

"You're clever," Grimbol's voice came from deep in the gloom.

"Not clever enough, either." Drest hung from her ropes, her ears tingling. She had come so far, so close, and failed at the final moment—but only through the betrayal of a man who had pretended to be her friend. "I'm Drest the Foolish."

"Nay, lass," Grimbol said. "That you came all this way past dangers on the road *and* entered this castle shows your courage. What shall I name you?"

"Drest the Fearless," called Wulfric in his great booming voice. "Call her that."

"Nay, call her Drest the Bold," said Gobin.

Uwen stuck his heels against the wall and leaned forward on his ring so that he could see her. "Drest the Daring. We can be Wild and Daring together."

"If you want a sneaky edge to it, Drest the Cunning," said Nutkin.

On the wall past Nutkin, Thorkill sighed. "I just think of her as our own dear Drest. Can we call her Drest the Dear?"

A sob caught in the girl's throat. *Drest the Weak. Drest the Feeble-Minded. Drest the Trusting.*

Drest the Kind.

She stiffened her jaw. "I was only caught because I was tricked at the end."

The prison was silent.

The girl closed her eyes and swung her feet back in an attempt to curl up. Her boots stuck against the stone wall behind her.

And remained stuck.

Drest blinked. It couldn't be. No one could have made a prison wall like that.

She slid her boots up. They stuck again on the ledge made by the stones and their mortar. There was not just one ledge: The wall was full of them.

Drest grabbed the rope that bound her hands and, her toes holding her place in the mortar, rose enough to release the pressure around her wrists. Slowly, careful not to lose her ledge, she twisted until she was facing the wall. With her boots still firm in place, her fingers found a crack. Without a sound, Drest gripped the wet wall and, crack by crack, climbed. In seconds, she had reached the iron ring.

"Who tricked you, Drest?" Gobin's voice was quiet beside her, as if he'd been thinking.

Drest closed her fingers around the cold iron ring and pulled herself up. Her arms were sore, but a ledge beneath her feet held her steady. "One of the knights. I found him after they invaded." She leaned against the slimy wall and closed her eyes.

"Was he the one missing when the ship took us away?" asked Gobin.

"Aye," said Drest. "I was going to trade him. I was taking him wounded, see, all the way to this castle." She faltered. "I'd trade him for one of you and then we'd attack and set the rest of you free."

"All this time, you had the missing knight in your power?" Wulfric asked.

A laugh erupted from across the prison. "Drest, my lass," Grimbol called, "you are cleverer than we ever gave you credit for. Do you know who that was? The man you caught?"

Drest paused. "He claimed his name was Emerick."

"Aye," said Grimbol, "Emerick Faintree, young Lord Faintree himself. The old lord's son."

Drest nearly lost her grip on the iron ring.

That explained why the guard's face had changed when he had seen who lay in the wagon, and the haste to get him inside. That explained the talisman. And that explained the false friendship. It had been nothing but a careful ruse; he'd needed her to help him reach the castle. *His* castle.

And it had been *his* order to capture her family from the beginning. *His* order to have them hanged.

"Drest is the cleverest of us all." Grimbol's voice came deep from the far end of the prison. "She took Lord Faintree himself. You are truly Drest the Clever, my lass, and no one can deny it."

There was a chorus of "Aye" from all her brothers.

They've always been good to me, Drest thought. *Even if they pillage towns. They've always loved me. Unlike some people.*

Drest locked her fingers on the ring and vowed never to let go. She would not allow the thought of some lily-faced, slime-headed eel to make her lose the small advantage she had gained.

Her brothers had gone from "Aye" to gruesome descriptions of what they'd do to the young Lord Faintree if and when they caught him.

"He's a monster like his father," Grimbol muttered from the other side of the prison. "He wants to see our wee lass hang with the rest of us.

"Not if I can help it," muttered Drest. She began to pick at the knots. They were tight and it was hard to peel back the fibers.

Gobin whistled. "Would you look at our wee lass now. When did you get up there, Drest? Can you untie yourself?"

All the iron rings creaked as her brothers leaned out to see.

"I don't know," Drest said. "They're good, strong knots. But I'm trying."

"I wish I had my dagger to lend you," Gobin said.

"Aye, a dagger would help, but none of us have—" Drest

stopped. The knight who had beaten her had searched only her boots for a weapon. The dagger she had stolen from Emerick was still strapped on her belt beneath her tunic.

Clenching the fingers of one of her bound hands on the iron ring, Drest crawled farther up the wall with the other, step by tiny step.

"What are you doing?" called Uwen. "Do you have a plan?"

"Shut it, you rot-headed prickle fish," snapped Drest.

Her hand brushed against her tunic and then the belt itself. One more fold. She stretched her fingers, forcing out the numbness, and touched the soft leather sheath. Then it was in her hand. With the twisting rope burning at her wrists, Drest traced her fingers up until she felt the dagger and its metal grip.

Carefully, Drest slipped the blade free. Her heart pounding, her fingertips slippery, she pivoted the blade back bit by bit, until at last it touched the rope, then sank it into the fibers.

The ropes loosened on her wrists. In the next instant, they were gone, and the twisting strands and their heavy knot disappeared into the darkness below with a splash.

"Would you look at her," Gobin said. "She's freed herself. Our Drest has a knife."

Drest held the ring with one hand, the dagger with the

other, and looked out over her family. Their faces glowed with pride and hope. They were liars, cheaters, and brutes, but all of the best kind.

And she was one of them.

"There's my lass," Grimbol said. "Can you climb across to me? Cut my ropes and I'll open my trap. Then I'll open the rest of them from outside."

"Don't be frightened, Drest," Wulfric called. "You're a brave lass." He nodded encouragingly—just as he had when he'd been the first to show her how to hold a sword.

"These walls will be nothing to you. You'll creep upon them like a spider," said Nutkin, who had stood beneath the sea cliff and caught her when she was learning to climb.

Thorkill leaned forward. "Drest, lass, remember how you strung my bow this winter? No one thought you could, yet you did. You can do this just as well."

"You can do it, Drest," Uwen said. "Do it quickly before you lose courage."

"Drest will never lose courage." Gobin gave Drest a smile—the radiant smile that he'd always given her when he'd come home from wars. "Go on, Drest. Show us what you can do."

Drest took a deep breath, and laughed. "You're very kind, lads, but I've no doubt that I can do this." She was about to climb to Gobin's ring on her way to her father's, but stopped and looked up to the wooden trap above her own head. "How will you open the trap, Da?"

"Your dagger, lass. The trap is closed with but a bar in two slots. I'll push it up with the blade."

"Why don't I do it here with mine?" With her feet firm in their hold and one hand on her ring, Drest reached up. She had seen the bar in the trap from the outside: a flat metal bolt as long as her arm that extended across the center of the wooden door that now lay above her head. Light shone around the edges of that door, interrupted by the bar in two places on either side. The bar was resting in two slots, Grimbol had said, so she would need shove it up. But how? From one end? From the other?

From both, Drest realized, one at a time.

She stuck her dagger's point in the crack below the bar closest to her head, and pushed up.

"Your arm isn't strong enough," her father said. "Don't even try. You'll drop your knife."

Drest slipped out her knife and stuck it in the crack across the door, as far as her arm would reach, and pushed. "You don't know me well if you think that."

She brought the blade back, and jostled the point of the bar nearest to her again, then its other side.

And again.

And again.

And then—the bar scraped, and moved, and the trap-door seemed to spring up.

"I've done it," Drest said. "Now I push?"

"Put your dagger where it's safe," called Grimbol, "and aye, reach up to the trap and push. Watch for the guard."

Drest carefully bit the dagger's grip. With her jaws tight, she drove her free hand against the trap.

The wooden door flew open, the iron ring on its outside banging against the stone floor.

Drest crawled out, blinking in the light from the wall torches, the dagger's grip still clenched between her jaws.

A guard in chain mail was leaning against the wall, his eyes wide and fixed upon her.

Drest sprang to the next trap on the floor. On her knees, she thrust up its bar and yanked on its ring to tear it open, then reached down. With one hand, she grabbed Gobin's wrist, and with the other slashed his ropes.

The guard drew his sword.

Gobin slipped out and rose at once into a sinister phantom shape between Drest and the guard. "Free Nutkin," her brother murmured. "Then run to the end and free Da."

Drest pushed up the bar on Nutkin's trap, flung open the door, and cut her brother's ropes. She hadn't even moved aside when he sprang out.

The twins threw themselves at the guard, who by that point was running away.

Drest ran to the last trap. Her hands were shaking, but she soon had the bar out, the hatch raised.

"Good lass," said Grimbol, his fierce eyes upon hers. "As quick as you can now."

There was a shout in the distance behind her, and footsteps pounding on stone.

Drest cut her father's ropes and slid aside as the Mad Wolf crawled out.

Soon Thorkill, Wulfric, and Uwen were free. Grimbol stood in the middle of the hall.

"They're coming for us, lads. Make yourselves ready, but don't fight if you can avoid it; we've none of us eaten in days, and we're weak as snails." He nodded at each of his sons. "Join a battle-mate and spread all over this castle. Find your way out: through windows and down walls. Fetch cloaks or cloths or furs to hide your faces. Now go, lads, and we'll meet in the wood by the sea." He nodded at Wulfric. "You take Drest." The Mad Wolf grabbed his daughter in a crushing embrace, then slipped down the hall on silent feet.

The twins followed their father, then Thorkill with Uwen at his side. Drest watched them, her stomach filled with tingling pinches of worry.

"You come with me," Wulfric said. "You're my battle-mate today."

A muffled cry sounded from down the hallway, then silence.

Wulfric turned to the first stairway. Drest followed him up the stone steps, but faltered, her knees suddenly weak.

Her brother looked back. His fearsome face softened. "Are you feeling unsteady, lass? I'm here with you. I won't let anything hurt you."

Drest had imagined his presence by her side so often that it seemed unreal to have him there at last. Though she knew they had to hurry, Drest couldn't help herself; she grabbed her enormous brother as high as she could reach, and hugged him. His strong arms closed over her back and his corded beard tickled her cheek.

"I missed you," Drest whispered.

Wulfric's grip tightened, and it almost seemed he would lift her from the ground. "I missed you too, lass."

A distant clank and a muffled cry farther up the stairs told them that a pair of brothers was not far ahead.

"Blast them," Wulfric said. "That would be the twins. Da told them not to fight. Let's go on our way." As he turned, he sniffed and drew his huge, rough hand beneath his nose.

31

VENGEANCE

Grimbol's order had been to escape, but as Drest watched Wulfric disarm and then slay a guard who tried to stop their way up the stairs, a new order lodged in her mind: Find Emerick and seek her vengeance. She could imagine the young Lord Faintree, arrogant and stern, chortling over the talisman. He had made a dire mistake, and he would soon find that out.

"This castle is strange," said Wulfric as he led the way up past the guard's body. "There should have been a window or some other way out by now. Or a hall. If we see one, we should take it."

"Wulfric, I need to go higher. I need to find—I need to find Borawyn." *That* would be her weapon: the sword that had been her true companion throughout her journey. She wouldn't need Gobin's voice to urge her on now.

"You had Borawyn all this time?" Her brother's face crinkled in amazement. "You're a lass in a million, Drest. But you won't find Borawyn here; they're sure to have put it in the armory."

"Nay," she said, "Borawyn's here somewhere." *With Emerick.*

"We can't risk our lives for a sword," said Wulfric, then added in a quieter voice, "Not even that sword."

"May I look for it while you look for a way out? I'll keep where I can hear you."

Wulfric shook his head and was about to answer, but before he could speak, a single pair of walking footsteps sounded on the stairs ahead of them.

Seconds later, below them: a fleet of boots, and they were running.

"Blast." Wulfric had taken the sword from the knight he'd slain and now held it ready. "When you see the one coming down, duck under him, and fly up the stairs. Look for a way out, and take it. Don't wait for me. I'll hold back the ones below and find my own way after."

Terror flared in Drest. It was like the headland again, and she was helpless with no sword.

"Did you hear me, Drest? You're to run. Get ready."

The knight from above came around the bend in the stairs: an older man who blanched at the sight of the Mad Wolf's eldest son.

Wulfric lunged, forcing the knight to the side, making room—just enough—for Drest on the stairs.

Drest scrambled past the slumped knight: up the steps,

around the curves, the panic of the invasion at the headland flooding her—

The invasion that Emerick ordered.

—and then a window appeared in the curving stone
wall, and below it the sea. It was wide enough for Wulfric
and easily wide enough for her.

Drest grabbed the sill and started to climb over, but
stopped.

If she left Faintree Castle now, she would never return.

If she left, Emerick would never be punished for his lies.

*Never falter before yourself or the enemy. Accept no defeat:
Always fight.*

Drest drew her leg back from the windowsill. There
would be more than one window like that in the castle.

Where would a castle keep its lord? Drest raced up the
stairway, meeting no one, but finding no hint. She came to
an arrow loop and looked out at the bailey.

It was a stage of confusion. Guards on foot and men on
horses raced across the grass between overturned wagons
and fleeing people.

She pulled away and continued up the stairs, faster. The
steps grew smaller and pressed close to the wall. If she had
been carrying Borawyn, it would have been difficult to
wield it and even harder to fight.

There were no more guards, but each time Drest glanced out an arrow loop, she saw knights streaming across the bailey, pushing through crowds of villagers who parted for them like frantic schools of minnows.

She climbed past doors that opened to storerooms, then came to a nail-studded door off the stairs. She burst in with her dagger drawn, but the large, ornate chamber—with a tiled floor, white walls with blue patterns, and a massive bed mounded with rich weavings—was empty.

The search was taking too long. Before she knew it, her whole family would escape and she alone would be trapped inside. Drest took the stairs three steps at a time, clutching the wall for balance.

For a long stretch, there were no arrow loops, but at last she came to another window. Drest peered out to see what side she was on: the sea or the bailey. It showed her a rocky cliff above the crashing waves. It was neither a good place to jump nor climb. She had to go on.

A sleek black shape bolted past the window.

Drest leaned out and watched a crow rise to a stone arch above another window, where it uttered a fearsome *creea*.

It was Mordag; she was sure of it. And the crow was marking the place of an enemy.

⤛ 32 ⤜

LORD FAINTREE

The door was locked. From somewhere inside, Mordag's call rang above an unfamiliar voice. Drest dropped to her knees. With any luck, this door would be like the prison's trap. She thrust her dagger into the crack and slammed it up.

The unmoving bar shot an ache through her arm.

Mordag began a wild string of caws.

Drest held her breath and pushed again. It was as if she were pushing her dagger against a cliff.

Beyond the door, a shout exploded, followed by a crash.

Then Emerick's cry.

Hearing his voice sent a shock through Drest, then a new bolt of rage. She drove the blade against the bar and, one hand clasped over the other, rose from her knees, trying to funnel her motion into her arms.

The bar moved. Barely. Then more. Then it was lifting, and Drest threw all her weight against the door.

She fell into the room just as the metal bar hit the tiled

floor with a thunderous crack. Drest's dagger dropped from her sweaty hands and clinked after it.

"Drest!"

Tig—his face clean, his black hair tidy, in a blue tunic with black hose—seized her wrist and dove to the side. Drest followed as a knight slashed his sword against the door where she had just been standing.

"Get out of here!" he roared, yanking his blade from the spot where it had embedded in the wood.

The red-faced knight.

The lavish chamber had been turned upside down, the tables flipped, the curtains around the bed slashed into wavering pieces. An alcove with a wide window that hung open to the sea lit the far wall, and against it hunched Emerick, his face shaven and pale. He wore no hose, only a long white tunic that was torn at the neck.

Drest and Tig scrambled out of the way of the knight's next blow, which crashed against the tiles. Her dagger was just inside the door, out of her reach.

"Did you hear me?" bellowed the knight. He went for her, but she was quick and feinted toward the door, while Tig clambered back.

"Where's Borawyn?" Drest shouted. "Where's my sword?"

"Out the window and in the sea," said the knight, and

laughed. "That's where you'll go too, if I don't catch you first!"

He came at her again. Drest dove to the side and grabbed the nearest object—an iron candlestick almost as long as a sword—and blocked the knight's blow. Thick yellow candles rattled over the floor. Drest had done well with her unusual shield; the knight's surprised eyes showed her that.

She blocked his sword at her feet, then at her head, each with a resounding clang. But though she was forcing him off and damaging his blade, Drest knew she wouldn't last long with such an awkward defense.

Behind her, Tig tried to crawl to safety. The knight saw the boy's movement and rushed for him.

Drest didn't have time to run; she threw the candlestick at the knight's knees. It struck him hard, and he fell with a crash. She grabbed Tig's arm and lunged toward the alcove.

Directly beside Emerick.

Drest turned to the red-faced knight, who had kicked away the candlestick. "Give me your sword! *I* will slay him!"

The knight laughed. "I don't know who you are, boy, but I'll give you some advice: Cherish this moment, for it will be one of your last." The knight began to stalk toward her.

"Drest," said Emerick, his face twisted. "Is that what you truly want? Revenge?"

"Is that not fitting? I protected you and saved your life and you—you *lied* to me."

A gust from the window chilled Drest's head, and she glanced out. The sea lay below, but so did a bed of rocks; she could see the foam around their points.

The knight gave another laugh. "The window? If you wish, boy, you may throw him out upon the rocks and jump after him." He stepped closer.

Drest straightened. Her life was now at risk.

Never falter before yourself or the enemy.

Accept no defeat: Always fight.

"You should cherish your own last moment," Drest told the red-faced knight. "And you've the brain of a minnow if you can't see that I'm a lass. I'm Grimbol's youngest, his only daughter, and I'm his most powerful weapon. I'm a legend, see."

He charged at her, but stopped and gave a cruel laugh as Drest recoiled. "A skittish weapon."

Drest's fingers tensed on the wall behind her—and brushed over a faint ledge in the stone.

It was same kind of ledge she had found in the prison, the ledge where the stones and mortar met.

The whole castle had been built with such ledges.

Drest gave the red-faced knight her most insolent smirk, despite her thundering heart. "Sometimes you need to waver to make the blow strong. But you wouldn't know that, would you; you're not just a traitor and a coward but a toad-faced boar's bladder."

He let out a booming laugh. "Do you think yourself brave to call me names?"

"Nay, everyone should call you names. You're a craven pile of fish-guts and you smell like them too."

The knight's eyes narrowed. "I'm coming for you, Grimbol's daughter, and I'll end your legend for good."

"Is that what you think? You've a head like a pig's stomach and it's full of the same muck." With her fingers on the wall, her legs ready to leap, Drest waited.

He lunged.

Three seconds.

Two seconds.

One second away from running her through.

Drest turned and leaped into the window, grabbing at the stone bricks above it on the outside, and yanked herself up.

Just barely avoiding the blade that plunged after her.

It extended through the window, glittering in the sun. The knight's arm followed, then his head as he stared at the cliffs below.

"Up here," called Drest. The sea wind tugged at her, but her holds were secure. "See if you can get me." He wasn't out far enough for her to dislodge with a sudden movement, but if he reached out more, he might be.

Growling, with a scrape of chain mail, the knight pushed his shoulders through. Now most of his weight was at the top half of his body. If she could make him lunge for her, he might slip.

Only—

The knight was crawling out, his feet on the window's sill, one hand on the stones, finding ledges just as Drest had, the other holding the sword aloft.

And now Drest was within his reach.

Trapped.

The knight raised his small, cruel eyes to her and his sword began to sweep up on a relentless path that in seconds would strike and knock her to the rocks below. "Farewell, Grimbol's daughter."

But as he finished his final word, the knight's eyes changed—from triumph to terror.

The power in his swing had dislodged his balance, and his feet were no longer on the sill. With his sword in one hand, his other hand alone could not support him.

With a howl, the red-faced knight fell—down into the sea's hungry maw.

← 33 →

THE LEGEND BEGINS

Drest was dizzy and her fingers numb, but her grips were strong on the castle's ledges. For that moment, she was safe from the pull of sea and stones below.

"Drest," came a choked voice. Tig's face appeared in the window.

"I'm up here," Drest said. "I'm coming down."

She had never climbed so carefully. Foot over foot, hand over hand, clinging to each ledge until she was sure she had the one below. Soon she was at the window, and she slipped inside.

"You really *are* a legend." Tig clamped his hands on her arms. "I can't believe what you just did. He could have killed you."

"He wasn't used to being on a cliff side—or a castle-side, and they feel the same to me. Balance is everything—that and your grips."

She was trying not to look at Emerick. He was on Tig's other side, breathing hard with the catch in his breath that meant he was in pain.

She was in the chamber now, her dagger by the door. It would take little to reach it and complete her goal.

But then Drest looked at Emerick.

His eyes were wet.

"Did he hurt you?" She cleared her throat.

"Does it matter?"

Drest pointed to the window. "I didn't lie; that was the man who pushed you into the ravine."

"That was Sir Maldred, my uncle Oswyn's most trusted man. Drest—I didn't intend for this to happen. I forgot about the talisman. If I'd remembered, I'd have asked for it back. I gave it to you when you were only Grimbol's daughter, and I—I—why didn't you wake me at the gatehouse?"

"How could I have woken you when they took you away? Aye, one of *your* guards made the wagon go on and the other had me in ropes. Was I to run after you? What would he have done to me if I'd tried?"

She tore herself from Tig's hands and stalked to the other side of the room to where Emerick's dagger waited. She picked it up. This would be a fitting weapon to enact her revenge. This was the weapon that would make it clear whose daughter she was.

But at that thought, dagger in hand, Drest hesitated. She'd just seen what Wulfric had done to the guards in his path.

Was *that* what she was?

A hot realization branched through her: She could not do it.

Drest slipped the dagger back into its sheath and pivoted to face the young lord.

"You always said my family are bloodthirsty villains," Drest said, "but you're the villain. Still, I'm going to spare your life. You saved mine once, so this is my payment for it."

"Oh, Drest," he whispered.

"I'd better go. All my brothers and my da are surely gone by now."

Tig stepped toward her. "You rescued them?"

"Aye, all of them, just as I told you I would. We're meeting off the castle grounds. Tig, do you want to come with me, or do you want to stay with him?"

The boy sighed. "Do you even hear yourself?"

Drest snorted. "I wish you farewell, then. You too, my *lord.*"

Emerick propped himself up by the window. The wind from the sea whipped his white tunic about his bare knees. "Would you have told the truth, Drest, if our places had been changed? You would have slain me in the ravine if you had known who I was."

She flushed. "I'm not a beast now, and I wasn't a beast then. Nay, Emerick, nothing would have changed. Only

I wouldn't have trusted you. And I wouldn't have liked you."

A series of cries came from the window by Drest's shoulder.

She looked out. A long line of carts and people on foot were hastening past the nearest gatehouse. There was no sign of her brothers.

On the inner battlements, one knight stood shouting orders. He was older than Drest's father, thin as a dead tree, with a slick of gray stubble for hair.

"Who's that?" Drest said as the old knight turned. His eyes met hers and did not look away. "Do you see him? He's giving orders."

"That must be my uncle," said Emerick in a hollow voice. "Has he seen you?"

"Aye."

"Then you'd best go swiftly, before they close the portcullis."

Once more, she looked at Emerick.

"Go, Drest," he murmured. "Before it's too late."

But she couldn't move. Something held her back: an ache that filled her chest. If she left that chamber, she would leave Emerick forever.

And leave him to die.

"He's after you, Emerick, isn't he? Not the war-band, but

you." The noise of the crowd below bubbled up through the window.

"He was my father's brother," Emerick said softly. "If I die, he becomes Lord Faintree. And no one in this castle will mind that."

The resentment that had filled her suddenly broke, like a branch that had carried too much weight. And with that burden gone, her head cleared.

It was Emerick—not the lord of the castle or the knight she had met in the ravine—but simply the young man, her friend, who stood before her.

"You need a guard," Drest said, "someone who can protect you from men like him." With the same flush of happiness she'd had when her brothers had returned home from war, she marched across the room to Emerick's side, the side she had always supported. "I forgive you. So come with me again, and I'll protect you."

Emerick looked sick. He looked old. He looked as if he could barely stand.

"That offer is more generous than I deserve," he said finally, "and I am grateful for it. But you must go on your own. Both of you. I would only hamper your escape."

"Nay, you won't hamper anything." Drest pulled his arm over her shoulder and reached around his waist, careful of his rib wound.

"Don't risk your life trying to save mine, Drest. I betrayed you. I lied to you. I'm the one who ordered your family's capture. Just *go*." His arm squeezed, then lifted.

But Drest had made a decision and it felt right, and real. It was one she would never regret.

Drest nodded at Tig. "Fetch Merewen's cloak. There it is, by the door. We'll wrap ourselves up in it."

"Drest, please," Emerick moaned. "Tig, can you take her?"

But Tig had already dashed across the room and had the cloak in his arms. "We'll look like an old woman with a bent back, and no one will notice us in the crowd. Will you come with us, my lord?" Tig held up the cloak. "I have a feeling you don't have much choice."

"I shall pick you up and carry you out of this castle if you don't come willingly," Drest said. "So don't try to fight me."

Emerick sighed. "I know better than to try that."

A hunched old woman in a black cloak staggered through Faintree Castle's Great Hall and stepped aside as a pair of knights raced past her toward the stairs leading back up into the keep. Other knights thundered by her to the nail-studded door that led out to the bailey. Two children were tucked beneath the old woman's arms, and she leaned upon them, the folds of her cloak hiding most of their figures.

At the grass the old woman became a part of the crush of villagers who had come to see the Mad Wolf hang and were hastening to leave the castle now that the Mad Wolf's war-band was roaming free. The old woman passed beneath the eye of Sir Oswyn Faintree, but he was too busy watching his nephew's window to notice her.

Drest could not support Emerick and walk quickly without drawing attention, so she stayed beneath his arm and walked at his pace, though every instinct screamed at her to run.

She kept her eyes down as they passed through the first gatehouse, focusing on the stones beneath her feet, the limping man in front of them, and the wagon just ahead. Two thin bearded men were sitting in the back of the wagon. Drest's gaze flicked over them—then back again. They were watching her closely. Something in those eyes was familiar. When they smiled, she recognized them: Gobin and Nutkin in disguise.

Drest tugged Emerick and Tig forward, never taking her eyes from the wagon and her brothers in their false black beards. Past a man on a donkey that shied at her approach, past a cluster of pilgrims, past a sheep wandering confusedly on its own.

"Old mother," called one of the bearded men—Nutkin—and waved his hand. "We thought we'd lost you."

As in a miracle story Grimbol had once told, the people before them parted. They saw an old woman supported by two children, and sympathy overcame their fear.

Gobin and Nutkin jumped down and lifted Emerick aboard the wagon as it moved on while Drest and Tig scrambled up. Drest sat between Emerick and the other villagers who had packed in for the ride.

Gobin leaned toward her. "We're in a wagon of purse-thieves. It's the safest place ever; no one's asking questions." He looked at Emerick and Tig. "Who are they?"

"No questions," whispered Drest. "I'll tell you later."

The wagon rattled past the second gatehouse. Drest remembered the guards who had seen her, and hid her face among the folds of the cloak.

Then the wagon was flying down the long bridge of earth over the sparkling sea and the crashing waves.

The twins sat motionless until they reached the cross-roads. When the horses slowed to turn, Gobin and Nutkin slipped out of the wagon, pulling Emerick down with them. The other travelers glanced as Drest and Tig followed, then looked away, and returned to their conversations.

So many travelers were hurrying that no one paid attention to the two bearded men, the two boys, and the hunched old woman who crossed the road and disappeared among the trees.

⊷ 34 ⊶

THE MAD WOLF'S WORLD

Gobin the Sly and Nutkin the Swift carried Emerick between them through the woods. Drest kept close, remembering what the twins had said in the prison about what they'd do to the man they were carrying: something about crushed bones.

They stopped to wait for Grimbol far from the road. The twins peeled off their beards, which they'd made from a black boar rug they'd found in someone's chambers. With their own scraggy stubble and their damp black hair pushed back from their faces, they looked older than Emerick.

"So who did we just carry?" Gobin said. "Will you tell us now?"

They were sitting in a small clearing, Drest, Emerick, and Tig in a row against a fallen tree. The twins were facing them, their long legs outstretched, their dark tunics and hose mixing with the shadows. That was one of their tricks: to blend into darkness, to disappear, to creep unseen upon the enemy.

For the first time, Drest noticed how sinister her favorite brothers looked.

"If I tell you, do you promise to do what I say?"

The twins exchanged a grin.

"That depends," said Gobin.

Drest's eyes narrowed. "I just rescued you from a prison. You owe me."

"Fair enough." Gobin winked at his twin. "But only if Nutkin agrees."

"Come, Drest," said Nutkin, "let's not play games. The knights will be after us before long."

Drest rose to her knees. "Listen well. This is Emerick Faintree, and I am his guard. If you touch him, I will slay you."

All mirth disappeared from the twins' faces.

"You *cannot* mean that," Gobin said. "Not any of those things."

"They're all true. I'll tell you why sometime, but for now you must trust me." She nodded at Tig. "This is Tig. His father is the miller at Phearsham Ridge. He came all this way to help me rescue you."

Mordag, who had been sitting on a branch behind them, swooped down to his shoulder.

"I would call this an honor," said Tig, "if I didn't know what kind of bloodthirsty brutes you were. I can say that, you see, because she's *my* guard as well."

A choked sound came from Gobin, but he controlled

himself. "So you've brought enemies among us, Drest. I don't know what you're thinking, but it's madness."

Tig reached up and stroked his crow. "We told her that too. But legends like her don't have to listen."

Disbelief shone on the twins' faces. A questioning look darted between them. It was clearly the nub of a plan, and likely an evil one, but then Emerick spoke.

"I have a proposal for you," the young lord said slowly in a muted version of his castle voice. He was hunched against the fallen tree, the huge black cloak spread over his legs and feet. "If anyone's going to murder me, let it be your father. But let me have a word with him first."

Across the clearing, Gobin rose. "I accept your proposal, lord. Da would want us to save you for him anyway." He paused. "You've a nasty prison in your castle, but a good, solid figure in your frame; I could feel it as we carried you. Too bad you have to die. We could have used you in the war-band."

Emerick's face became bitter. "Is that a compliment? Do you think I would ever choose your war-band over death?"

Nutkin stood and gestured for Drest to come. She hesitated, then scrambled up, leaving Tig at Emerick's side. Each twin slipped an arm around her and drew her away through a patch of slender hazel trees just beyond the clearing.

"Your *friend* the lord doesn't have manners," said Gobin, "though we've just saved his life."

"Your own manners are none too golden," retorted Drest.

"Look at our wee Drest, defending the enemy." Gobin's arm tightened around her. "We're not angry with you, lass. You came to save us, and you still stand here as our own sister." He leaned down and kissed the top of her head. "But you should take better care with how you choose your friends."

"How would you know about friends?" said Drest. "You haven't got any; you go about raiding villages and stealing people's goods, so everyone in the lowlands hates you. That's why there was such a crowd to see the hanging."

The twins stopped walking.

"I'm not sure I heard you say that," muttered Gobin.

Drest looked from one to the other. "Did you ever burn a village when it refused to pay you tribute? Was it called Yettsmoor?"

"Oh, but we had to," Nutkin said. "You wouldn't understand."

"What about that red linen we have at home? Did you steal it from a place called Weemsdale?"

Gobin shrugged. "You've known about us, haven't you?"

"Aye, but—what about all the Weemsdale maidens you kidnapped?"

The twins frowned.

"That," said Gobin, "is a filthy lie. We have never laid a finger on a maiden and never will."

"Lass," said Nutkin, "you know the code."

"I know the code, but someone told Emerick—"

"What would you say if we told you it wasn't *all* the maidens of Weemsdale but only five, and they'd followed us?"

Nutkin nodded. "And they said they'd follow us wherever we went unless we gave back their fathers' weavings. What would the code have us do with them?"

Drest looked at her brothers. Their faces were serious. "I don't know."

"It would have us spare them," Gobin said. "We bound them and took them back."

"They were humiliated," Nutkin added, "but not hurt. Not one maiden in that village was hurt."

The twins withdrew their arms from her shoulders.

"Let this be a lesson for you," said Gobin. "You can't always control your legend."

Thorkill the Ready was the next to find them. He had climbed down the keep, down that terrible cliff, and swum all that way, and was soaked and tired. His face brightened at the sight of Drest, but the brightness faded when Gobin told him who Emerick was and that they had to wait.

The twins went off to look for the others. They returned with Uwen the Wild and, not long after, Wulfric the Strong and Grimbol the Savage himself. The Mad Wolf's sons congratulated one another on their successful escape and each gave Drest a long embrace. The twins must have told them about Drest's companions, for every one of them ignored Tig, who stood with his arms crossed near Emerick, and cast only swift, hostile glances at Emerick, who watched them from a distance with wary eyes.

Grimbol, however, did not embrace Drest when he walked into the clearing. His gaze fixed on Emerick alone. Without a pause, the old warrior stepped past his sons to stand before the wounded man.

Everyone stopped talking.

"Gobin said you have a word for me," growled the Mad Wolf in his gravelly voice. Slowly, he drew a dagger from his belt. He held it blade-down. "I have a word for you too, but you go first."

Drest darted away from her brothers and knelt beside Emerick to help him sit up. She didn't want to look at her father. She knew she had to find a way to stop what he was about to do, but her mind was blank.

"What are you doing, Drest?" said Grimbol with a frown. "Did you not bring him here for me?"

"Nay, I saved his life. Leave him alone, Da."

The Mad Wolf's eyes grew hard. "Get away, Drest. Don't question me."

She was about to answer, but Emerick spoke first: "Go."

Tig grasped her hand. With a lump in her throat, Drest let Tig pull her away.

The Mad Wolf settled back on his heels. "Go on, lord. Say you what you want. Then it's my turn."

Emerick's jaw stiffened. He spoke with his haughty castle voice, though it was also ringed with pain.

"For most of my life, I've thought of saying these words to you, Grimbol. I know my father wronged you, but you took the wrong revenge. If you wished to devastate him, you'd have done better to murder me, not Celestria. *I* was his heir. You may have thought you'd destroy him by what you did, but he cared little for his daughter. Did you never know that? I was the only one at the castle who loved her, and you destroyed only me: a boy, nothing more. You murdered a girl who loved you. So go on, murder her brother who hates you, and finish what you began."

The men of the war-band made a sudden movement, but they hadn't taken more than a step when Grimbol swung around.

"Stay *back*," he snarled. Then he swung to face Emerick again, the dagger still in his hand.

I am not like him, Drest thought, her eyes following her

father. The words were distinct in her mind. She made a sudden wild decision: She would throw herself in the path of her father's blow. She slipped her hand from Tig's.

"So that's the story you heard." Grimbol clenched his dagger.

"It's not a story." Emerick shuddered. "I saw Celestria that night, after you were gone."

"Would you like to know the truth, lord? What really happened?" The Mad Wolf grimaced. "*I* didn't slay her. I saved her. I tried."

Emerick's eyes did not leave his.

"You knew what her fate was supposed to be: marriage to Lord de Moys. I don't care that he was your father's ally; she was but a wee lady and he was a filthy coward three times her age." Grimbol's voice was hoarse. "She was afraid of him. She sent me notes, begging me to rescue her. Of course I came. I climbed the tower and brought her down. Aye, to a boat on the rocks with a lad from my war-band, my best sailor. But someone saw us. I gave her to my lad and told him to sail. I went back to fight. Five knights, all falling on me with their swords. I fought as I'd fought on battlefields. They saw again what I could be."

Drest sat back on her heels and stared. She had never seen such misery on her father's face.

"She was brave, my wee lady," he went on. "She would

not go with the lad. Nay, though he held her, she slipped free like a fish and came back to where I fought. She came back to save me." His eyes now gleamed wet. "And as she did, your own knight slew her. Sir Maldred. The rest were aiming for me."

He told more: how he'd lashed out in rage and slain the knights who stood watching, stunned by what Sir Maldred had done. Sir Maldred escaped, climbing a rope that had been let down from a window in the castle, and began shouting for reinforcements. Grimbol had been ready to climb after him, but his war-band lad had torn him away, taken him to the boat, and set sail.

"I don't know why Maldred did it, lord. To put everyone against me? I've been thinking all these years, and that's the only reason I can see." Grimbol paused. "Before I left, I picked up my wee lady in my arms and took her in that boat. I was going to bury her in a place that only I would know. But then I thought of you. That's what made me bring her back to where she had fallen. I knew that you, her brother, should see her buried, not I."

Emerick had not said a word. Tears were streaking down his cheeks.

And down Grimbol's too.

Drest could barely breathe past the swelling in her throat.

Grimbol lunged toward the young lord, dropping the

dagger on his way. He gripped Emerick's shoulders with both hands.

"I did not slay Lady Celestria," he said in a slow, ragged voice. "I loved her as if she were my own wee lass, and she knew it. Do you know it, lord? Do you understand it now?"

Drest could not take her eyes from her father. He was holding the young lord as if there were no difference between them, as if brutal warrior and noble knight were one and the same. As if this man were his son.

The woods were silent around them.

And then Mordag flew up into the sky, circled, and returned with a series of hoarse caws.

Tig turned to Drest, frantic. "Enemies—more than four, from her calls. It must be the knights."

Drest scrambled to her feet. "Tig's crow is never wrong. We have to run. Come, Emerick, I'll carry you."

But Grimbol drew the young lord to his feet before she could reach him.

"Gobin, Nutkin," the Mad Wolf called, "take him between you, and take him with care. All of you, listen: No one shall hurt this man. He's Celestria's brother, and he's one of us."

⊷ 35 ⊷

RETURN TO PHEARSHAM RIDGE

The war-band sprinted through the woods, but the landscape would turn into fields soon, Grimbol said, and would no longer hide them. He and Wulfric ventured out onto the road. With all the people leaving Faintree Castle, stealing a cart would be easy. And within minutes, a sharp whistle came. The two were waiting in a covered wagon with two horses; the old driver and his son had stopped for a necessary trip to the trees, and the sight of the Mad Wolf and *his* son had been enough to send them bolting.

Before other carts rumbled past, Wulfric and Thorkill leaped onto the bench in the front, Wulfric grabbing the reins. The rest of the war-band squeezed into the back, pushing aside sacks of grain, heavy sloshing tubs, and rolls of coarse linen.

The wagon began to move with a jolt.

Uwen wedged himself beside a tub and the twins propped up Emerick on the linen rolls. Tig settled by the young lord, and Drest started to join them, but her father grabbed her wrist.

"I want a word with you, lass."

She sat beside him near the sheet of wood that hung over the opening, and waited.

"You're my own dear girl," he said, his voice harsh against her ear, "and I wish to the stars that I could keep you safe. But it's time for you to be one of the war-band and take your place among your brothers. You're braver than all of them put together, you know."

Drest sighed. "I don't want to be brave all the time."

With a faint smile, the Mad Wolf drew his daughter into his arms, as if she were still small, and rested his chin against her hair.

"You have to be brave now, lass; the knights are after us. We must keep running. We'll take your wee friend back to Phearsham Ridge, then go north for supplies and news, but not stay long in any town. We'll keep to the woods until the hunt for us dies." He gave a short chuckle. "Before we do."

The journey to Phearsham Ridge was fast by wagon. Drest had been dozing when the wagon stopped. Seconds later, the back opened and a gust of fresh air flowed in.

"Out," Grimbol said as his sons struggled to wake. "Every last one of you. We don't know what we'll find here, so I want you all to be ready."

After the twins and Uwen had emerged from the wagon,

Grimbol climbed back and watched Tig's futile attempt to draw Emerick to his feet.

"He's half dead, isn't he," the Mad Wolf said, his voice quiet with tenderness. "Come, my lord. We can't have that. Up we go."

Drest watched as her father gently hoisted Emerick to his feet and carried him out.

The night air was bracing in its cold, yet fresh and clean, a relief from the stuffiness of the wagon. But Drest didn't pause with her brothers, or with Tig, who stood apart, whispering to Mordag. She darted over to where her father had propped Emerick against a tree and was under the young lord's arm in her usual position just as he began to crumple.

"Thank you," he murmured.

Gobin sauntered over. "I don't think Da needs us yet. Shall we take him from you, Drest? It's just up ahead, lord."

"Nay, I'll carry him," Drest said. "He needs to go slowly. He needs the air."

"Aye, we all do. What a stinking trap that was. We smell none too sweet, but I think one of those barrels was rotting."

Drest bit her lip. She had smelled the stench of rot as well and had only just realized where it had come from: Emerick's rib wound. It hadn't smelled like that before.

Grimbol gathered his sons and bade them start toward the village. He hung back with Drest.

"If you need one of us, raise your voice, but keep back. I cannot promise how this village will welcome us." Grimbol grabbed Tig by his shoulder. "You, lad, will come with me to the front."

"Da, I need Tig—"

"*I* need him up here. We don't know how many villagers came to the castle to watch us die, and if we'll need to fight, he's our token, our safe passage. Come, lad. No one's going to hurt you unless you struggle."

With his hand firm on Tig's shoulder, the Mad Wolf drew ahead, and soon Drest and Emerick were alone. Her brothers' tall figures were but shadows on the road before them.

Drest looked up at Emerick's haggard face.

"I'm sorry," Drest said.

"I know," said Emerick. He stopped to cough, and bent over with the pain. "Drest, I've misjudged—"

"You shouldn't talk; that will hurt." Drest winced at his rasp as he inhaled. "Keep your breath for breathing."

"I must speak while I still can. I may die like this on your shoulder." He swallowed with difficulty. "I've misjudged—what you've had to face in your life. You are an extraordinary person. None of what happened—is your fault. And

I'll always be grateful—that I've known you. Drest, please forgive me—everything."

And then he was coughing again, unable to stop, his whole chest shaking, his hand against his ribs.

"If you die on my shoulder after all we've been through," Drest said, her throat thick, "I'll never forgive you."

They rounded the next bend. The Mad Wolf's band was far ahead, nearly to the mill. The river gleamed in the moonlight.

But a huge figure stood on the road between Drest and her family. It shifted, becoming two, then three: one tall figure and two large ones.

"Is that you, child?" Wimarca's voice cut through the darkness.

Relief washed over Drest. "Aye, it is, and I've got my friend Emerick here, and he needs—"

"I know," the healer said. "I've been collecting night herbs in the woods, and I heard you come. I've called on two farmers to carry him."

The two large figures advanced and knelt, laying a long wool blanket on the ground.

"Set him there," Wimarca said. She was wearing a cloak of sea-green wool that smelled of wood. "Take him to my hut."

The two men cast Drest a curious glance, then took Emerick from her shoulder and laid him on the blanket. They lifted each corner, and Emerick's body rose, swaying faintly between them.

Drest went to the healer's side. "What can I do for him?"

"Nothing, child. Go with your war-band."

"You won't let him die?"

Wimarca set a gentle, dry hand on Drest's cheek. "I will tend to him as if he were my son. Now go, child, and help your family. If your father treats this village as an enemy, it will become precisely that."

Drest looked at Emerick. His eyes were closed, but he was breathing. With a nod at Wimarca, Drest turned back to the road and broke into a run.

And ran as she had not run since she had left the headland.

← 36 →

SANCTUARY

Grimbol was pulling Tig by his shoulder through the square when Drest came up beside him.

"I know the miller," said Drest. "I'll call him for you, Da."

Without waiting for her father's leave, she sprinted ahead to the familiar building. But before she reached the door, it opened and Arnulf's old face looked out.

"You're back." His gaze slid over to the war-band. "You've brought your family."

"Aye," said Drest, "and it's thanks to you for letting me take Tig. He's been a world of help. Da, this is Tig's father. Arnulf, this is my da. This is Grimbol."

Grimbol approached with Tig, his eyes narrowed. "Aye, I know him."

"It's been years since we've met, sir." Arnulf stared at Grimbol's scarred, rough hand on Tig's thin shoulder.

Silence but for the splash of the water wheel.

Tig struggled beneath the Mad Wolf's grasp. "You should have seen it, Father. This warrior maiden freed the lot of them from the depths of the castle prison. We truly have a legend in our midst."

"Do we?" murmured Arnulf, his face unchanged.

Grimbol's fingers must have loosened, for, with a sudden jerk, Tig was free from his hand. "And I've legends behind me too. Phearsham Ridge will be rich with stories." He whirled on his heel and bowed to Grimbol—just out of his reach. "Let us give food and beds to *these* legends, who are weary from their travels and unjust imprisonment."

"Aye," said Grimbol. "We need one night, and then we'll go on."

Arnulf's hand closed on Tig's shoulder, and he drew him close. "Come inside, sir, and my lads and daughter will serve you."

Soon the whole war-band was in the mill's big room. The miller's family rushed about, serving meat and ale. But each time Idony or Wyneck passed Tig, they stopped to squeeze his shoulder, as if to be sure he was real.

Drest yawned, and sank before the cold hearth. She looked up at the rafters where she had hidden, then at the corner where Emerick had stood with Tig.

She was with her family again in the very room where she had spoken about their rescue, but at that moment, she did not feel like joining them.

She had changed.

"What's wrong with you, Drest?" Uwen thumped down at her side. "You're sitting all quiet over here by yourself."

At his words, which echoed throughout the room, the rest of her brothers set down their food, their faces concerned.

"Her bruises must be paining her." Gobin marched over and reached down to trace the bruise on Drest's cheek. "That guard didn't spare her one bit. How I wish I'd hunted him down."

"Did he strike you on your ribs?" Thorkill lumbered toward her and knelt. "Lift your tunic, lass, and let me see."

"Nay, my ribs are fine." Drest crawled away from them, against the wall. "You're all breathing too hard on me."

Nutkin slunk after her and grabbed her hand. "What's this on your fingers? From climbing? Look, lads, there's dried blood at their tips. Who has water?"

Drest pulled her hand away and held it between her knees. "My fingers always bleed when I climb; you've never looked before."

"She's shaking," Uwen said in amazement. "Our Drest is shaking over here." Then, pleading, "Drest, what's wrong?"

"She's seen more strife in this one day than ever in all her years." Wulfric walked before her. "It's likely to stun a wee lass. Take a nice, slow breath, and then tell us everything."

"Your crowding close is likely to stun me—you all smell like rotten fish. Will you give me room to breathe?"

Grimbol pushed his way through his sons until he stood beside his eldest—shorter by a hand, but Wulfric stepped away at once, giving him his spot.

"Does she have to ask a fourth time? If it had been any of the rest of you, would you even have had to ask twice?" He turned and glared at each of his sons. "The lass has traveled for days with her wounded battle-mate, got a sound beating, freed us, then had to escape. Do you think she might be tired? Do you think she might need a rest—not just to close her eyes, but a rest from talk of fighting? We'll be in the middle of it again soon enough. Let her find her peace tonight."

Grimbol watched his sons retreat and then dropped to his knees beside his daughter. "Are you brooding, lass?"

"Nay, I don't brood. That's for Thorkill."

Her father laughed. "Don't let him hear you say that."

Drest settled back. She'd had many questions to ask her father, and most had been answered. Except for one. "Da? Did you ever know a bandit named Jupp?"

"Jupp?" The old warrior's eyes widened. "Where have you heard that name?"

"He's a man I met on my way." She thought of telling her father how Jupp had chased her, then decided against it. "He told me to tell you that he's still loyal."

"So you met Jupp," Grimbol murmured. "That lad—he was the sailor I'd taken to help me rescue my wee lady."

"Your most trusted lad," Drest said softly, remembering her father's words. Then she shook herself. "Da—he told me you poisoned his town."

The Mad Wolf took a deep breath. "Aye, lass, that was my punishment for him. He'd not followed his order; he'd not taken my wee lady away in the boat. That was our plan if anyone saw us: He'd take her and I'd stay to fight. But he waited for me, and let Celestria get away. That's how he betrayed me. There are tricks that you learn when you fight for a castle, lass. I used them on his village."

"But to poison a whole town—"

"I only made the well unclean, undrinkable, so no one could live there. It would be an empty village, a punishment for him and a tribute to my wee lady. I thought it would help me go on. And yet, my lass, some nights I regret it. What good did it do? My lad Jupp was the youngest of the war-band I had before your brothers. He'd always been loyal. From what you say, he still is, bless him."

"Da," Drest whispered, "people died in Birrensgate from that water. Jupp's sister and her bairn, and more."

"Nay, they didn't. Not from that well."

"I was there, Da. I saw the stones in the doorways. And Jupp told me."

258

Grimbol stared at his big, rough hands in his lap. "I didn't mean for that to happen. I didn't mean for his family—ah, Jupp, poor lad." He sighed. "Even your old da makes mistakes, lass. And this is one that will haunt me."

Drest put her hand over her father's.

The old warrior took a long, deep breath. "Where is Lord Faintree?"

"The healer took him." Drest paused. "What will happen to him, Da? He has enemies in Faintree Castle. Like his uncle. And they'll be hunting him."

A subtle change came over Grimbol's face, a new, thoughtful look. "Oswyn?"

"Aye, Da. He sent that Sir Maldred to slay Emerick. Twice." She paused. "He's the knight I sent off the castle's cliff."

Grimbol stared. "My own wee lass? We trained you better than I knew."

"Maybe you did, or maybe it was just me. But we have to think of Emerick now. That Oswyn wants him dead."

"He's become bold," Grimbol murmured. "To send a man like Maldred to slay the lord in his own castle—he's sure of his support, sure he won't be punished."

"Aye, Da. So Emerick can't go back. And we can't leave him alone here, either."

"Let me think, lass. With luck, we can stay here for a few

days, maybe even a fortnight. I see a solution before us, and Oswyn is at its center, but reaching him—that will be the problem. But you're right; we can't leave your battle-mate behind."

The old warrior kissed his daughter, and let her go.

Drest sat back and watched him walk ponderously to his sons. He had listened to her—as his daughter, brave and strong in her own right, and as a member of his war-band. And he loved her—of that she had no doubt.

Much later that night, when her father and brothers were settled around the big room's floor, Drest left her blanket and slipped outside with Tig.

"What was it like for you in the castle?" Drest asked. "They were beating on me when they took me in, and I didn't see much of anything but the floor."

"It was beautiful. The paintings on the walls, the carved stone everywhere, the rich cloths all the servants wore—" He stopped. "They didn't hurt me, but they led me aside for questioning. Two burly guards and that traitorous knight. I'm sorry; I pretended I didn't know you."

"Nay, I don't blame you. They'd have put *you* in ropes too, if you'd told the truth."

Tig gave a little bow. "Thank you for that. By the by, I

lied to them about everything: I told them I was the brewer's son from Soggyweald and had been helping Emerick ever since he staggered into our town. I also told them that my name was Drest, but my casual name was Tig—so if Emerick asked for one of us, there wouldn't be any question—" He broke off. "I wasn't trying to pretend I was you, Drest."

"You wouldn't have done very well if you had. I *am* a legend, you know." She pointed at his rich blue tunic. "They gave you fine clothes. Did they give you a post at the castle?"

"No, they sent me to Emerick. He'd been asking for Drest. He was frantic with worry, and when he saw my face—he—he looked as if I had murdered you."

Drest laughed. "Well, you *did* steal my name."

Tig did not smile. "No one knew where you had gone. Emerick called for a squire and made him look for the farmer to find out. I had the idea to ask the guards, and when the one who'd caught you came up to his chamber—you should have seen Emerick. There he was, still wounded—a woman had shaved his face and bandaged his shoulder, but not his ribs yet—and he—he flew out of his bed and grabbed that guard's shoulders, hauled him to his feet, and cried, 'Find that boy and take him to me now, or I'll see you hanged!'"

Drest stared at Tig, who was watching her expectantly.

"That's a good story," she said, "but he's too wounded to have done that. What did he really do?"

Flushing, Tig looked down. "It *was* a good story, wasn't it? But very well, if you must have the truth. When the guard said you were in prison, Emerick fainted. And he didn't wake up until that knight came to kill him."

"Sir Maldred. He's the one who murdered Emerick's sister, Lady Celestria. And no one knows why." Drest glanced at the river, which was flowing rapidly, turning the water wheel on the mill behind them. The splash was comforting, almost like the waves at home. "Can you take me to Emerick?"

They went past the river to a path through the trees and to the stone hut in the small clearing where Tig had stopped many days ago. Mordag joined them when they reached it, and landed on Tig's outstretched arm.

"We'll stay out here," Tig said, "Mordag and I."

Drest pushed open the hut's door and crept in.

A pot sat on a crackling fire in the center of the room, and, from a stool, Wimarca stirred it. She nodded toward the back wall. In a bed festooned with fragrant herbs, Emerick lay sleeping, his chest rising and falling smoothly, his face at peace.

Drest went to his side. The rotting smell was gone, replaced by a clean and herbal scent. She knelt and touched his hand.

His eyes fluttered open. "Drest?"

"Aye, I'm here. Your wound's been treated at last, has it?"

"Yes. I feel no pain. I feel very little." His words were soft. "Wimarca gave me something quite strong to drink."

"Maybe it will help you sleep. You deserve a good sleep, after all I've put you through."

A weak smile rose to his lips, then faded. "Do you forgive me, Drest?"

"Of course I do. Do you forgive *me* coming in to murder you?"

His lips twitched. "I'm grateful that you came in to murder me; if you hadn't, Sir Maldred would have done it. Just as he murdered Celestria."

Tears filled his eyes.

"Though perhaps it would have been best if you hadn't come. Or at least you should have left me. I can do no good in this world, Drest, and will always draw danger to those around me." He shuddered. "They're hunting me. All my knights. They won't stop until I am dead."

Drest leaned close. "Emerick, if Jupp could be loyal to my da, there have to be *some* loyal men at your castle."

"They're all loyal, but to the past. Most of my knights

have followed Oswyn in battle. Many of them were with him on Crusade." Emerick was trembling. "I shall never see my castle again. There is not one man in this world who is loyal enough to protect me."

"Aye, but there's a lass." Drest squeezed his hand. "I'm not leaving you, Emerick. When I said I was your guard, I meant it. Don't even think of doubting me."

The young lord turned his hand up to grasp hers. "Of course. There is not a knight truer or more chivalrous in Faintree Castle than you, Drest. I could not ask for a better guard."

"And friend. I'm your friend too, am I not?"

"I could not ask for a better friend." Emerick swallowed, breathed, and started to speak again, but something caught in his throat. He shook his head.

"Get some honest sleep, lad." Drest started to rise.

His weak grip tightened. "Don't leave yet. Please."

Drest settled back on the floor beside the bed, her hand still in Emerick's.

She watched the young lord's pale blue eyes close, then closed her own eyes and rested her head on the blanket by his arm.

Drest told herself to not think of the knights streaming from the castle in chase of her family, nor the home that Emerick had lost, nor her new role in the war-band. Emerick would be safe with her brothers around him, and her whole family would stay in Phearsham Ridge until he was well. And no knights would bother with that sleepy little town so far from Faintree Castle. They might not even remember that it existed.

With that comforting thought, Drest at last drifted to sleep—deep, blissful sleep as she had not experienced since she had left the headland.

Code of the Mad Wolf's War-Band:

Shuttle your courage back and forth
with someone you trust.

Always carry a weapon.

Never falter before yourself or the enemy.

Accept no defeat: Always fight.

Honor and protect all matrons and maidens.

Wulfric's Three Rules of Battle:

Prepare yourself with weapons.

Control your anger as its own fine blade.

Get your rest, and stay warm, for the field will be cold and
you will often need to draw on the memory of that warmth.

Drest's Code:

Sometimes words alone can save your life.

⤙ Glossary ⤚

Arrow loop: A narrow opening or slit in a castle's wall or battlement, used to fire arrows from within.

Bailey: The inner yard of a castle, between a defensive wall and the inner tower.

Bairn (pronounced *BERN*): Scots for "child."

Battlement: The top of a castle wall or tower, usually featuring spaced openings through which its warriors fight.

Crenellated: Used to describe a piece of stonework, such as a battlement, with thick square pieces (merlons) with wide gaps (crenels) between them.

Crossguard (part of a sword): A horizontal piece of metal on the hilt just above the blade that protects the hand on the grip.

Curtain wall: The defensive outer wall of a castle. There can be more than one.

Demesne (pronounced *de-MAIN*): The lord's share of crops, designated as specific sections of a field. In feudal societies, lords own many individual towns and villages, and the people of those places pay to live there with those crops.

Grip (part of a sword): The middle part of the hilt between the pommel and the crossguard; it's what you hold.

Hauberk (pronounced *HALL-berk*): A shirt of chain mail that covers the neck, shoulders, arms, and chest, and reaches past the hips.

Helm: A helmet, part of a knight's armor that protects the head.

Hilt (part of a sword): The entire top section of a sword (everything that comes above the blade itself).

Hull: The underside or body of a boat or ship.

Inner bailey: The fortified inner wall of a castle directly before the tower or keep.

Keep: The inner building or tower of a castle, protected by outer fortifications, and thus its safest place.

Pommel (part of a sword): The shaped end of a sword's hilt, which sticks out beyond the hand and serves as a counterweight.

Portcullis: A gate made of metal or wood (or both) with a series of spikes across the bottom. It slides between two grooves in a gatehouse, raised and lowered from within. It's an essential part of a castle's defense.

Surcoat: A long, loose, sleeveless garment worn over chain mail, reaching the knees, usually with a heraldic emblem on the front (Faintree Castle's is a blue tree).

⤙ Author's Note ⤚

*T*he *Mad Wolf's Daughter* takes place during a period of relative peace in medieval Scotland. By this point in history, Scotland found itself a poor country (compared to England), yet a strong one. England was a natural aggressor, but Scotland was far enough north, remote enough, and fierce, and hadn't been easy to subdue. So English kings and Scottish kings came to an agreement: England would technically be in charge, but Scotland would have its own king and system of autonomous government.

In 1210, that agreement was in full force, and Scotland was near the end of the reign of William I. He was an old man who could look back at a reasonably successful kingship: Law and order and town life had grown beneath him, as had feudal society, and there was stability overall. The country was experiencing a long, peaceful lull, although on the horizon, Scotland would be the site of a series of famous battles that would define its identity.

I didn't write about famous battles, or royalty, or any famous people. I wanted to depict the kinds of ordinary people around whom local legends would spring. To this end, all my characters and their conflicts are fictional. But they're based on history.

Feudalism and Village Life

Lord Faintree's relationship with the villagers reflects the feudal society that existed in the early thirteenth century. Villagers were officially tenants, and, to pay for the privilege of living and working in the village, had to tend the lord's demesne. This was a section of land that villagers planted, farmed, and harvested along with their own. Villagers were assigned to work in the lord's demesne on certain days each week or month, and had no choice, which could mean neglecting their own crops.

Mills, like the one Arnulf manages, could be another source of income for the lord: By requiring villagers to grind their grain at the village mill and not at home, the lord could demand a portion of each share of milled grain. The miller would collect these shares by the lord's order, as well as his own shares. (Millers were not always well liked in their villages and were often the richest people in town.) Arnulf clearly cares about his fellow villagers more than the money he can make from them, and is as eager as they are to throw aside Lord Faintree's control. If Phearsham Ridge had been a real town, its remoteness might have helped save it: Faintree Castle would have been too busy with its other towns, and with wars, and the small amount of grain from the fields and the mill wouldn't have been worth the manpower.

Villages also paid their lord through their residents themselves, providing men to fight in the lord's wars—though they were untrained, armed with their own weapons (spears and knives), and often had only wool or leather armor or no armor (chain mail was expensive and worn only by knights). This was the "brute force" part of the army.

Knights like Sir Maldred might live an honored life at a lord's castle, but could also have owned land. Knights were always subjects of their lord, like villagers, and paid their dues through their own (and their villagers') military service. Knights who didn't personally lead their own men in battle were considered cowards.

Small war-band invasions of towns and settlements weren't unusual during this period, particularly in the Scottish Borders, the region of Scotland that directly abuts England. Knights or lords might send a war-band over to pillage, often as part of a larger act of aggression. Grimbol would have served in such a war-band and learned its ways.

War-Bands

Different kinds of war-bands existed during medieval times. Some war-bands were part of a formal army. Grimbol served in a formal army when he fought for Faintree Castle, and, like other men-at-arms, lived at the castle. Some men-at-arms might live outside in one of their lord's villages. Grimbol's later war-bands (such as his war-band with Jupp, for example) were different. Composed of outlaws, the members in those war-bands often did not live in the same village, but generally lived as normal people did—in houses, and might have even been tradesmen. When Grimbol formed a war-band of his sons, he gave up a so-called civilized life in exchange for one of constant training—though *his* war-band doesn't have the luxury of sleeping in beds or under roofs. They sleep outside on the beach, armed and ready to rise at a moment's notice. In poor weather, they crowd into the sea caves, which isn't too comfortable. For his family war-band, Grimbol set up a life like the one he must have known when en route to a battle for Faintree Castle.

Women

Idony, Wimarca, Celestria, and Merewen show some of the varied levels of freedom that matrons and maidens had in medieval society, often more than you might think.

In villages, unmarried or widowed women could own property and have jobs like blacksmith, miller, carpenter, and more. But while women could do what were considered men's jobs, they often didn't; there was a great deal of daily backbreaking household labor—laundry, food preparation, and cleaning—done by hand and with limited supplies (think fat, lye, and ash for soap). Women typically took this on, and also helped with the farming.

A noblewoman like Celestria would have had a different life. She could inherit, but only if she didn't have a brother. Yet her father had complete control over her future and could dictate whom she married, even if she hated the man. Noblewomen were often used as pawns in political games, their marriages forming family alliances. While she would have been taught how to behave at court, as well as read, weave, and heal, she would have also been taught that obedience to her father or husband was her greatest virtue.

Girls like the two in Launceford had more freedom than just about anyone else: Living on the street, survival was more important than gender roles. They would have been asked to steal, along with their brothers. Yet like many children in their situation, if they couldn't earn their keep, they would be seen as just more mouths to feed.

Few maidens would learn how to fight with a sword like Drest, yet some learned how to use other weapons. Longbows were the popular option for maidens to learn, especially in castles. That's something that Drest and Celestria would have had in common.

Healers like Wimarca, Merewen, and Elinor (Tig's mother) might choose to remain unmarried to retain total control of their lives. Yet that made them vulnerable to a village's whims and ire, even as they played such an important role. Most women knew basic healing techniques, but a dedicated healer was special.

Healing

Medieval medicine wasn't perfect: yarrow, for instance, was said to help heal wounds; and gillyflowers could cure paralysis. But astute healers knew effective remedies, such as willow bark, which contains a substance like one prominent in modern painkillers, to soothe pain. Some medieval concoctions included what we know today as poisonous plants, but a tiny dose could work wonders, and a good healer would know how to use them.

Castles

Medieval castles of this period were built in the Norman style: hulking stone brutes with rectangular towers, surrounded by stone walls. These were considered modern castles. Not long before the thirteenth century, castles were built in the motte-and-bailey style: a mound of earth with a wooden tower (the motte) surrounded by a grassy space and a wooden fence (the bailey). Those castles were easy to burn and didn't last long in sieges. When William the Conqueror came up from England in the late eleventh century, he began building stone castles—and so did the Scottish lords and knights who sought to defend their lands.

A strong defensive castle would have at least one gatehouse, a wall, and a stretch of land between the wall and the keep. Castle defenders used crossbows, which could penetrate chain mail and were very easy to fire.

Castles often had more than one kind of prison: one for noble prisoners, which was in a tower with windows and light; and one for commoners lower down, in a pit. Prisoners in the first type could expect to eventually leave; they might have been defeated on a field of war and were being held for ransom, so it was in the lord's best interest to keep them alive. Prisoners in the second type, though, could expect to perish in their prison. That Faintree Castle planned to execute the Mad Wolf and his war-band *outside* of the prison (rather than simply letting them starve) shows that its rulers were willing to go to some expense and trouble for their revenge.

There is no castle like Faintree Castle in Scotland today. There may have been a similar castle once, but the famous Scottish warrior king Robert the Bruce would have probably destroyed it; during his lifetime, he saw many Scottish castles taken over by English forces, and so when he gained them back, he tore down the castles to prevent that from happening again. I always feel sorry for those ruined castles.

Swords

In just about every medieval movie battle, you'll see a dramatic clash of blades between characters. And that's where movie battles go horribly wrong: No warrior in his right mind would do that to his sword (at least not before the two-handed claymore, a fifteenth-century weapon).

A sword was an expensive piece of weaponry made of steel, a specialized and pricey metal. A sword that met a shield or chain mail would just need to be sharpened. And that was expected. But swords that met other swords would get nicked, and that was bad (or broken in half, which was even worse). To repair a nicked blade, a swordsmith would need to sharpen the edge down until the nicked part was gone. Do that enough times, and you no longer have an edge. That's now a pretty useless, expensive piece of weaponry. A knight would always try to dodge a blow or use his shield to block it; that's why each of the Mad Wolf's sons sleeps beside his shield. (Drest doesn't carry a shield because there aren't any left on the headland when the knights depart. Even if she had found one, it would have sunk in the sea.)

The Landscape

The setting for *The Mad Wolf's Daughter* is a fictional Scotland. It takes liberally from the Scottish Lowlands, a historic region that encompasses the southeastern coast and the Scottish Borders, goes west to Dumfries and Galloway, and reaches up past Stirling, and then to part of Aberdeenshire.

There is no coastline in Scotland that looks like the route between the Mad Wolf's headland and Faintree Castle. There are, however, rocky beaches and cliffs up the east coast that are reminiscent of the headland and Faintree Castle's natural defenses. And there are many spots of woodland that, combined, would replicate the landscape along Drest and Emerick's journey. I adjusted Scotland's historical geography to fit the story. I hope my Scottish friends will forgive me.

The Characters' Names

Early in the novel, Emerick notes that Drest's name is that of a savage Pict. All the characters' names stem from specific cultures of the region, but Grimbol's children bear names that hint at war or invasion, and history.

Wulfric and *Thorkill* are, respectively, Germanic/Saxon and Nordic (think Northmen or, as many people like to call them, Vikings). Those were two cultures that invaded and helped to shape Britain in the centuries before this novel takes place.

Gobin comes from *Gobert*, a Norman name (another invading culture), and is a diminutive. So is *Nutkin*, for *Cnut* (another Northman name, and also a warrior king of England).

Uwen comes from the Pictish *Vuen*. The Picts were the people of ancient Scotland. They were known as savage warriors and were the main reason that the Romans built their wall.

Drest comes from a whole lineage of Pictish kings: There were ten of them named Drest, from 412 to 848, and their names might have been spelled *Drest*, *Drust*, or *Drost*. Yes, Grimbol gave his daughter the toughest name of the lot.

Diane Magras, Maine

⊷ Acknowledgments ⊶

Writing a novel is a journey rife with danger. I am grateful to the brave souls who strapped on their sword-belts, grabbed sacks of provisions, and kept by my side on the way.

There were those who were crucial from the start. Thank you to my son, Benjamin, my first reader and editor, who has read and critiqued every draft. At the very beginning, you urged me to take the risky but exciting path at the cliff's edge. You always posed incredible questions, and never stopped helping me perfect those cliffhanger chapter endings. Thank you also to my husband, Michael, my next reader. You read draft after draft and told me what you honestly thought of each one. Along this journey, you pushed and supported me. I am grateful to you both for always believing in me.

Thank you to my incredible agent, Adriann Ranta Zurhellen, whose suggestions and advice helped me to pull this novel out of the waves and onto the cliff-points to which we really could cling; and who found me my perfect editor, Kathy Dawson. Kathy, your questions and suggestions challenged and inspired me to race up to the highest point of the highest cliff. Thank you for never letting me take the easy trail. You regularly gave me the flush of courage that I needed to go ever farther.

I am immensely grateful to Antonio Javier Caparo for putting his extraordinary imagination and skill into the work of art that is my cover. Thank you, sir, for interpreting Drest so perfectly, and creating such a work of art to draw readers into Drest's world.

Thank you to the whole team at Kathy Dawson Books and Penguin Young Readers: in particular, Susie Albert, Claire Evans, Maggie Edkins, Regina Castillo, Mina Chung, Judy Samuels, and Lily Yengle.

To my critique partner Anita Saxena and to Casey Lyall and Salma Wahdy: Thank you for reading drafts, sharing advice, and being stalwart supports and friends along the way. To the Freeport Community Library, the Maine State Library, and all the Maine libraries that are part of the Minerva and MaineCat networks: Thank you for providing the crucial resources I needed during my research. Special thanks to librarians Mary Lehmer and Joanne Libby, and librarian/teachers Julia Colvin and Lynne Perednia for their support, enthusiasm, and friendships. Many thanks as well to Nicole Rancourt and my other talented colleagues at the Maine Humanities Council for the same.

To my parents: Thank you for giving me own vast granite headland in which to grow up and for filling my young life with books. And to Mom: I wish you could have been here to see what this story has become. Your positive outlook even in the darkest times spurred me to write the tale of Drest. She would have loved you as much I do.

THE LASS IS ON THE RUN!

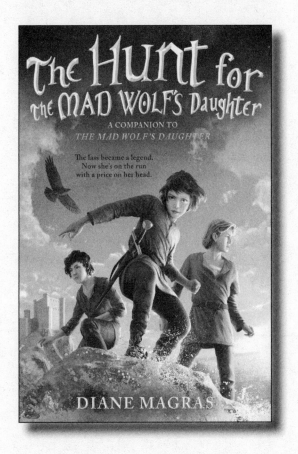

Keep reading to see where she goes . . .

◄-‹-›-►

part one: the bounty

⤛ 1 ⤜

THE NEXT MORNING

A crow's shattering *creea* sounded beyond the healer's hut from somewhere on the village path.

"Did you hear that?" Drest bolted up from the floor, thumping her shoulder painfully against the heavy wooden bed. "That's Tig's crow."

"Was it one call?" Emerick, the injured knight—nay, *lord*—who had been her companion for the past six days, sat up and pushed away the blankets. "Or was that two? Drest, can you defeat two enemies?"

She reached up for the dagger sheathed against her ribs. "I can try."

"No, what am I saying? I'm half-asleep." He wiped his fair hair from his sweating forehead. "Will you help me up? We must hide in the woods." He tried to swing his legs over the bed, but stopped, seized in pain.

Carefully but firmly, Drest pushed him back onto the bed. "Nay, we don't need to hide. Mordag was only waking you, Emerick. She knows how well you heal when you're woken in the night and need to flee." She patted his bandaged chest. "This is nearly as good as being on the road, is it not?"

"I have my soundest sleep, of course, when I'm woken every few hours fearing for my life." He wet his lips. "*Was* that one call, or two? Where's Tig? Has he not heard his crow's warning?"

"Tig's at the mill and he's surely heard it. But if you like, I'll go out and see what's there." Drest pointed to Wimarca, the village healer, who was sleeping by the circle of embers in the center of the room. "Wake her if you need her."

"*If* I need her? Drest, there is surely someone out there. Mordag doesn't make that call for nothing." Emerick grabbed her arm, his grip surprisingly strong, though it trembled. "You've not slept for I don't know *how* many days. You've barely eaten. If you try to challenge anyone, you'll fall. Drest, you're weak as a kitten—"

"A wolf cub. I'm as weak as a wolf cub who smells its prey." Gently, Drest pried his fingers from her arm. "And if I find someone, I'll slay him, or hide from him, or mock him. I'm good at that, see. And I'll be back before you know."

Emerick frowned. "If Mordag is warning us of knights again, you must run. Run where they cannot find you.

Wimarca can help *me*, but *you* must go, as swiftly as you can. If they catch you, they'll kill you this time."

Drest scrambled away from the bed, no longer in Emerick's reach. "Are you worried for me? Strange. I *am* a legend, and I seem to make it through anything that tries to set me back. I've saved your life twice. I intend to do it again."

"Thrice," Emerick said gloomily. "You've saved my life thrice." He sighed. "Please be careful."

"I always *am*."

She bowed low, then slipped to the door and outside.

THE TERROR OF THE WOODS

Drest trotted away from the hut and into the woods, her jeweled dagger now drawn. It made her feel strong, though a sword at her hip would have made her feel better. Once she was deep among the trees, she listened, then went on. She brushed past leafy branches, over mossy stones, as silent as the mist that shrouded the night around her.

Each time she'd heard Mordag's call for the past week, an enemy had been near:

A bandit on the dusty road.

A knight with his sword raised in a castle chamber.

An army of castle men streaming into the woods after her family.

The crow called again: a lingering note of warning. It was louder now, and close.

Drest shivered in her thin tunic with its ripped-off sleeves. The night was cold and damp. All around her, the trees formed monstrous shapes, their branches weaving above her head to block out the sky.

And there she was, sleep pulling at her consciousness like a stone in a net, alone in the woods.

Alone. Yet not alone: Her father and brothers were resting at the mill, ready to leap to their feet with their weapons.

But they didn't *have* their weapons, she remembered: All their swords had been broken or taken from them when they'd been captured at their headland home. Her family had hung from iron rings in Faintree Castle's prison for five days. The only weapons they would have would be the ones they'd stolen during their escape.

Nay, but our hands are our greatest weapons yet, said a rumbling deep voice in her mind: her eldest brother, Wulfric. She had long imagined her brothers' voices when she had been alone before. Wulfric's voice softened the edge from her fear.

Perhaps we've all heard Mordag as well, came her favorite brother Gobin's voice, a smile in his words. *You know what that means, do you not, lass?*

We'll be prowling, said his twin, Nutkin. *The terror of the woods.*

Drest shook her head. They had never been prowling in real life when she'd imagined their voices like that, which meant that she was still alone.

The best you can hope for is your lad Tig. The voice of Thorkill, her second-eldest brother, was thoughtful and calm. *He's heard his crow, and he'll come out to see what she's calling about.*

The best you can hope for is to dig up your own courage wherever you've buried it, you mewing squirrel-brained fish-gut, sneered the voice of Uwen, her youngest brother.

Drest searched the trunks around her for the twins' black-haired phantom shapes, or the towering figures of Wulfric or Thorkill, or Uwen's smaller one.

But there was no sign of them.

Nor of Grimbol, her father, the Mad Wolf of the North—who would have ordered her to wait for the warband and not go out alone.

I may be alone, but I'm not frightened, Drest thought. *I've seen my family captured by enemies, been under a bandit's knife, and hung from a ring in a dark and horrible prison. These are only woods.*

Another call from Mordag, harsh and desolate—from the other side of the village.

Near the mill.

Where all of Drest's family were sleeping.

Drest broke into a run, her pace long and swift, toward the faded echo of the call.

She emerged into the hay field at the top of the village, a sea of murky green in the dark. Stalks whispered beneath her feet as she skirted the edge.

6

Soon she was at the town square by the mill. That squat building with its wheel on the stream was but a deeper shadow in the night.

Silence. Not even wind.

Yet Mordag had called from the mill. The crow had never been wrong before. Something was surely out there.

Drest started to cross the dusty square, her eyes on the mill. Nothing was moving. The shadows were motionless.

Halfway there, Drest shot a glance down the grassy path that led to the villagers' huts.

She froze.

In the center of the path stood a knight. Even in the dark, his chain mail hood seemed to glimmer as he turned toward her.